# About the author

This is my first published novel, although I have written three. I live in Tucson, Arizona with my partner, Lori. We have been together twenty-two years. We have four great kids, Rachel, Sara, Autumn and Justin. Our passions are traveling and our six-year-old grandson, Gavin. We have a little rescue dog named Chloe and a tank of constantly reproducing fish. If I don't become that accomplished writer I dream about becoming, I suppose I can always open a tropical fish store.

This is a work of fiction. Names, characters, businesses, places, events and incidents are either the products of the author's imagination or used in a fictitious manner. Any resemblance to actual persons, living or dead, or actual events is purely coincidental.

# LURKING IN SHADOWS

# INA E. SHICOFF

---

# LURKING IN SHADOWS

Vanguard Press

# Dedication

This work is dedicated to my partner, Lori, who has never failed to believe in me, and to dear friends who encouraged me to revisit old manuscripts that inspired me to create new ones.

# Acknowledgements

This book would not have happened without Don Weise and his belief in me as a writer. I owe you a bottle of vodka.

I would like to thank the team at Pegasus Elliot Mackenzie Publishers for their ongoing guidance and humor throughout this first-time publishing experience, and for finding all my misplaced commas, typos and spelling errors.

Justin Lonsway for his technical savvy and amazing patience.

Autumn Cleveland, thank you for making me change out of a t-shirt and shorts to make my cover photo look presentable.

Ray Cleveland, your photography is amazing and I'm honored to have it on the cover of my book.

Thank you to Rachel and Sara for their love, honesty and generous encouragement.

Thank you comes from my heart to Lori Stadler, for your love, enthusiasm and support for twenty-three years. Enduring my moods and impatience on a daily basis does not go unnoticed by me.

"Behind every strong woman is a story that gave her no other choice."

Nakeia Homer

Ann had been looking forward to attending the seminar. Tucson in October was her favorite time of year. The evening air reminded her of growing up in California, where evenings still cooled down, even in summer. She loved Tucson and her life here. She had the sexiest woman in the world to come home to, and a psychiatric practice with her best friend since childhood, which gave her satisfaction knowing she was making a difference in people's lives. Life was good. How could she know that this perfect October evening was about to change her world and how she saw herself in it?

The piercing pain between her legs flooded her head with white light. Ann opened her eyes and the light shot through her pupils to the back of her skull. Glaring down from the garage ceiling beam was a pendant lamp attached high above her. She tried to move her arms to shield her eyes, but she couldn't. That's when the reality of her situation invaded her with the memories of the last few torturous hours. Her body screamed with renewed pain.

She lay spreadeagled on a thin wrestling mat that had been casually tossed on a concrete floor of a giant warehouse garage somewhere in Tucson or Green Valley, at least she thought she was still in Green Valley. The last thing she remembered was getting into her car after the seminar there, and then blackness and silence. Her wrists and ankles were bound with tire strips, attached to stainless steel rings anchored to the garage floor. He had slammed her head down on the thin mat; unfortunately, she regained consciousness. Odd how the smell of his stale cigarette breath was her first recall of him. Her second memory was his mocking face a few inches away from hers. She tasted her own blood and remembered the savage bites to her lip and inner thigh.

Suddenly her nightmarish recall was diverted to the woman next to her, similarly bound, moaning softly. Her face was badly swollen and bruised. The woman's blonde hair was streaked with her own blood. Ann's stomach lurched at the sight of teeth marks that had been sunk deeply into the woman's breast. She too had been viciously raped, by evidence of drying blood smeared across her inner thighs.

Ann tested her wrist restraints. They were securely in place, as were her ankle ties. She painfully raised her head to study her surroundings more carefully. That's when she saw what was to be her and her fellow victim's fate. Near the corner of the garage, discarded like roadkill, was an oily tarp partially draped over the body of a woman.

The massive metal door of the garage clanged as it opened wide enough to allow him to drag in his next victim. He looked even larger than Ann remembered. He was over six feet, muscular with long dirty hair that swept across his unshaven face. Ironically, there was a large cross tattooed on the inside of his upper arm. He was laughing at the flaying woman as he was effortlessly dragging her into the garage. She was pounding him with her fists, which only seemed to make the moment more festive for him. He pushed her down on a mat next to Ann's left. Staring down at his newest victim, baiting her to attempt to escape. He sneered at her. The attractive brunette tried to regain her balance and he slammed a meaty fist into her chest, knocking the air from her lungs. He quickly tired of toying with her and reached down, ripping her blouse front from her body. He slowly removed his belt and pants. Looming over her, he smiled down at his captive. He sneered and said, "When I'm done with the three of you," motioning toward Ann, "you all are going to beg me to kill you just like that one did over there." He pointed to the cadaver's beaten and bloody body in the corner. Ann closed her eyes, her terror was visceral, knowing how she was going to die. She prayed the woman's screams and suffering would stop soon, but would her life as well? *Will I be next, or will he come back for the blonde first?*

*Someone, someone must be hearing the screams and come to our aid*, Ann thought. But no, it didn't happen that way.

Then… like in a fast-forwarded movie, everything happened quickly. The brunette had fought him with all the adrenaline left in her body. Sexually spent, he laid atop his victim with his head close enough to Ann's bound hand. In pure desperation, she grabbed his hair close to the scalp and held on even as his arm crashed across her shoulder and neck, sending lighting through her head once again. In that split second, the newest victim somehow found one more ounce of strength. Not yet tied down, she got out from under him, kicked him in the head, and grabbed a pipe wrench from the worktable behind her. With a baseball type swing, she struck him on the side of his head. His body went limp against the mat. Without a moment's hesitation she found a hacksaw and cut Ann free of her restraints. Both women quickly freed the blonde.

This was the first time the brunette had allowed herself to cry. Her whole body was trembling as the tears spilled out in release. Her voice quivered. "Do you think I've killed him?"

Ann was rubbing the circulation back into her wrists as she spoke. "Let's get him tied up in case he comes to." When they had him secured in the same fashion they had just been in moments before, they released the blonde and gathered up the remains of their tattered clothes and dressed in awkward silence. The blonde wasn't done yet. She picked up the pipe wrench returning it to the workbench as if she were tiding up her kitchen. It seemed such a surreal gesture to Ann among all the blood and gore.

Ann watched the blonde walk over to the dead woman and uncover her body from the tarp. She quietly stood looking at her. She reached down and picked up the knife he had used to kill her. Her hand gripped the handle of the knife with determined intent, as she returned to the man. Ann shuddered as she looked into the blonde's cold, steel eyes. She kicked him in the ribs, and he moaned. "Good. I thought she had killed you," she said. She kicked him again and this time he opened his eyes and looked up at her. She leaned over and spit into his face. Mimicking the words, he had used on her, "Beg me to stop," she hissed at him.

His eyes darkened in rage. "Bitch, you better pray you got the guts to kill me now or I'll find you again. Next time it will take you a very long time to die."

Ann and the brunette watched in horror, as the blonde raised the knife and systematically stabbed him repeatedly in his groin and stomach. The sound that came from his lungs was primeval, sounding like some wild animal. He strained against his bindings writhing in pain. Ann felt like she was going to faint. His blood had sprayed and pooling around his body. The brunette helped the blonde up from her knees after her attack had exhausted her. The three women exchanged looks, it was over, they had survived. In that brief moment they knew this horror would forever bond them. They made their separate escapes into the night.

# CHAPTER 1
## Karen Michaels

It was the first week of October and anything but a cold Tucson night. Nonetheless she shivered as she poked at her torn and bloody clothes, pushing them deeper into the flames of the fireplace. She looked down at her slim, firm body covered with bruises. Her wavy brunette hair hung around her face, streaked with blood prior to her first shower. Tightening the belt around her fluffy terrycloth robe, she tucked her legs under herself in Jack's easy chair and took a sip of her cappuccino. She thought, *Thank God Jack took the kids camping with his father for a few days.* She had showered twice since finding her way home and still she didn't feel clean. She wondered if she ever would again. She couldn't believe she was sitting here calmly drinking coffee like nothing had happened. She wondered if she should call the police. *Can they trace my call? I can't talk about what he did to me. They will know I witnessed a murder.* The phone startled her, and she spilled her coffee on her robe when she jumped.

"Karen, Karen, you there?"

"Yeah, Rita. It's me."

"I've been worried, where have you been all night?" Rita didn't wait for an answer. "What did you think of Sharon's dress tonight? Girl, it looked like two coyote cubs wresting under her slip all evening." There was silence for a fleeting minute. "I do not hear any laughing."

*Had the fundraiser really taken place earlier? It seemed like a millennium ago.* "Sorry, I have this monster headache. I came home and went straight to bed."

"I'm sorry I woke you. I called earlier and there was no answer. Swapping the dirt can wait till morning. Go back to sleep."

"Thanks, Rita, talk to you tomorrow." Suddenly Karen felt totally alone. Rita was an acquaintance, not a friend. She didn't have girlfriends that she could share this nightmare experience with. Her mother, well, she would only blame her somehow for causing it to happen. Ironically, Jack should have been the first one to think of calling. Sadly, she knew he would be the least comforting or supportive person in her life. *Jack emotionally left me a long time ago.* Karen looked down at her robe. *That coffee stain will never come out.* Thinking of this mundane spill on her robe suddenly made her cry. The pent-up fear, rage and pain finally flowed in a torrid release of tears and sobs. She removed her robe and stuffed it into the washer, pushing it down repeatedly in a frenzy of anger. She slid down the washer front to the floor and just sat there letting it happen. Her ribcage ached from the crying, *or was it from the bruises and contusions?* She looked down at her naked body, and softly touched the tenderest of her wounds. *How could this happen to me? I'm always careful and aware of my surroundings, especially in enclosed parking garages. It was at the country club garage for God's sake! Suddenly he was looming over me. How could anyone that big be lurking in shadows?*

## Addie Carson

Addie lowered herself slowly into the bath, trying to remember her abduction. Funny how you think of the stupidest things when they aren't important. *Did I shut the trunk of my car? I have been to the Tucson airport hundreds of times and many times at night. How can you be taken at an airport without any witnesses?* The only memory was his large hand over her mouth. He stunk like cigarettes. Then everything went black. What didn't ache, sting, or scream at her in pain was somehow comforted by the hot water. Tears slowly rolled down her swollen face, as the anger she had been trying to control started to surface again. *At least I finally killed one of these bastards! If I had killed all the men in my life that raped or abused me, I'd be a superhero for millions of women.* That thought actually made her smile.

With redirected anger, *I should be on my way to Aruba right now. I worked hard for this vacation, damn it! Two weeks on the beach will now turn into two weeks healing and hiding in this apartment until I resemble myself again. God I would have looked hot in that new bikini. Shit! I'll call Mom in the morning and tell her I arrived safely in Aruba. God, I can't believe this happened. I hope he's bled out by now. I should have made sure. Eventually someone will find their bodies. That dead woman, it could have been me.* Addie shivered in the heat of the bath.

# Ann Weiss

Ann sat on the couch wrapped in a blanket. She wanted to be in a hot bath but couldn't move in that direction. She looked around the room filling herself with familiarity and convincing herself that she was finally home and safe. The clock ticking over the mantle and their cat Coco curled up on her lap purring were familiar and reassuring sounds. She was finally safe. Ann was five foot three and no match for that monster. She weighed one hundred and fifteen pounds and must have felt like a Styrofoam cup when he lifted her off the ground. She had no idea how she had held onto his scalp so tightly after the brunette was raped. It was pure adrenaline. There wasn't a part of her body that didn't hurt as she slowly picked up the phone and starred at it a few seconds before dialing. "May I speak to Dr Nicole Chen, please?" Ann trembled slightly as she waited for them to page Nicky. *I can't tell her he was murdered.*

*No police report. I will be okay as soon as her arms are around me.*

"This is Dr Chen."

"Nicky, it's me. When are you leaving the hospital?"

"I should be out of here in a half hour. Honey, you sound weird, are you okay?"

Ann was determined not to lose it over the phone. "No. Could you bring an antibiotic home?"

Sounding concerned, she asked, "Why? What's up?"

"I got a bite."

There was a pause. "What kind of bite?"

"A human bite."

Nicky tightened her grip on the hospital's paging phone. "I'm on my way home."

## One week later
## Karen

It was harder getting out of bed each morning since that horrible night. Facing another day rehashing all the details was exhausting and almost as frightening as the actual event. Karen heard the shower and dreaded the thought of a confrontation this early with Jack. She rolled over with her back to the bathroom, hoping he would think she was still sleeping. He had returned three days after the rape, and he questioned her about her bruises. He didn't seem to be very concerned when she told him she had been mugged. What really hurt was she was sure his reaction would have been the same if she had told him she had really been raped. He merely suggested maybe she should see their family doctor. His uncaring reaction had not surprised her. Their cold relationship was ongoing now for months.

It seemed odd to her that the news hadn't reported the discovery of the bodies of a male and female in a Tucson garage. Could that possibly mean the bodies were still there undiscovered? The memory flashed in her mind as it did ten times a day and continuously at night. Tears flooded her eyes and she gripped at the blanket, pulling it up around her chin. The week had gone by in a fog and she was beginning to wonder if she was ever to wake up from this nightmare. She will just have to find a way to forget. *I know my own strength and I can do this.*

She had not heard the shower going off and suddenly Jack was in the room talking. "Do you think you can remember to pick up the kids from school today?" It was a snotty rhetorical question and he continued, "I'm sure you really could not care less how embarrassing it is to be called out of important client meeting to pick up my kids at the school when their stay-at-home-mom is probably out shopping with her phone off." He slammed the dresser drawer. He toned down his anger a notch. "Okay, listen. I'm sorry you got mugged and you're still sore, but maybe you could remember to pick up my shirts at the dry cleaners? They have been there for over a week." With effort, Karen climbed out of bed and headed for the bathroom. Trying to shut him out, she remained silent.

Jack reached for her forearm. "Are you listening to me?" Before he could touch her, she pulled away.

Bitingly she snapped, "Jack, leave me alone."

"Dammit, Karen. You have responsibilities. I work my ass off for this family."

She shot him a dirty look. "Please. You don't even know you have a family. You are too busy screwing your paralegal and impressing your law partner with the details."

He sighed and looked defeated. "Will you never let that drop? I told you it was over. I fired her. She's not even in the office anymore."

"God, Jack, do you really think I'm that stupid? You're already getting off on interviewing the next one."

He snarled at her, "I don't have time for this. I'm late, just pick-up the kids and my shirts." He started for the door.

Usually, she was less apt to confront him, but now threw caution to the wind. "You mean your shirts and then your kids. You do remember you have them. Oh, by the way, one of them is having a birthday on Saturday; you might want your secretary to pick up a gift for him, if you can remember which son it is."

He turned and spat out, "You know you are really being a bitch. If I can get them to school on my way to

work, the least you can do is pick them up from school."
Mindful of the distance between them, Karen turned her
back on him and walked into the bathroom.

Karen had been able to avoid her volunteer country
club work all week but knew she wouldn't be able to
continue doing so much longer.

The abduction and the growing problems with Jack
suddenly became overwhelming. She forced herself to
focus. *Do I want to stay and work things out with Jack?
Even if I do, will he be willing to try? Maybe focus on
that, and the rest will fall into place.* We used to be so
good, she remembered. She had met Jack at the
University of Arizona when she was a junior going for
her MBA. He was in law school and the most handsome
man she had ever met. He still was. He was full of ideals
and was determined to correct all the injustices in the
world. That was before his father let him know he would
stop paying for law school unless his major was
corporate law. He was to forget his foolishness about
the underdogs in this world and concentrate on getting
into a prestigious law firm and start making some
serious money. Jack buckled, after what seemed to
Karen a short period of time. But then who was she to
judge? She came from a family of old money that ruled
every aspect of her and her parents' lives. Her parents
only agreed to her attending the University of Arizona
to find a suitable husband. And she did. But to be fair,
she really did love Jack back then. He was kind,
thoughtful, and driven. They were happy and spent

every free moment together. Sex with him was always exciting back then. He was creative and took his time pleasing her. They would linger in bed and talk about anything and everything. When did that all change? Work became the number one priority, his second was being impressive to his father and father-in-law. Karen wanted to believe she was at least next on his list. In her heart she knew she wasn't. There was always something or someone more important to Jack. That's when she stupidly believed that a child would change him. Two children later only filled her days with the kids. She was busy with the boys, and Jack… well, Jack was still busy with Jack. So, was it too late or did it even matter anymore?

Karen crossed the plush bedroom carpet to the wet bar and poured herself a drink. She stared at the glass. It wasn't even eight in the morning. She poured it into the sink and entered the shower. Her bruises had started to fade from deep purple to yellow. She soaped up gently, her body still tender to the touch. She looked down at herself. She was still a very attractive woman. Even after the boys were born, her weight came off quickly after each pregnancy. Her breasts were still firm and perfectly proportioned to her slim and shapely body, even after breastfeeding the boys. In the first years of their marriage Jack would tell her and show her how much he loved her body. She still looked the same. *Wasn't she enough for him? Why did he need to sleep around with other women?*

She dressed, taking care to make sure her outfit covered all bruises. She went downstairs and cleaned up the scattered Cheerio's on the kitchen island from the boys' "self-made breakfast". After washing the few dishes left in the sink, she grabbed her purse on her way out. The time had come to confront Jack. She knew he wouldn't be able to walk away like he did at home when he didn't want to deal with their issues. She had no control of what happened to her the night of the rape. She desperately needed to regain a sense of control that would give her some assurance that she hadn't lost herself.

By the time she reached Jack's office she thought she knew what his response would be, pure indifference.

Lynn, Jack's secretary, was a well-dressed woman in her early fifties with an austere professional manner. Lynn had always been warm and kind to her and the boys, but Karen always sensed the look of pity in Lynn's eyes when she spoke to her. Karen saw that very look as Lynn greeted her. *How much more did his secretary know about Jack's affairs?* Karen wondered.

"Mrs Michael, how nice to see you. I'll let your husband know you are here."

Jack remained seated behind his desk and looked up at his wife. It had been a very long time since she had visited her husband's office. Confused about why Karen had made an appearance, he kept his court-room-poker-face. He waited for her to speak. Karen remained standing for a few seconds and then sat on the edge of his desk facing him. Behind him on a stylish mahogany breakfront sat an award Jack had received last year for the donation of uniforms made to their son's baseball team. That was one of the very few activities he involved himself with the boys, because it gave him city council accolades and great publicity photo shots. She picked up the family picture next to it that had been taken at Jack's parents' house for Christmas. It was three years old. She stared at it for a moment. She returned it to its position on his breakfront. Trophy wife came to her mind as she stared at herself with the perfect American family. Jack cleared his throat to break the silence.

She looked at him trying to figure out how to start. She decided to just be direct. "Jack… we are in trouble. We have been for a long time. Maybe it's time we think about marriage counseling." Jack was visibly flustered, an emotion he was not comfortable with; as Karen predicted, he would hide his feelings by rejecting the thought. He ran his fingers through his hair. "Jesus, Karen, if this is about the affair—"

"No, Jack, this about us. Don't tell me you aren't unhappy too."

Accusingly, he said, "I'm happy, it's you. You have been so distant and cold lately. If *you* want to go to counseling, I'll support you a hundred percent, honey." He stood and wrapped his arms around her. "Yes, I think that is a wonderful idea. No one has to know."

She knew once again he wasn't interested in their marriage, and certainly not being a part of making it work. She slowly pulled away, *God forbid anyone knows,* she thought. *How would that look?* Jack, like her parents, were all about appearances and secrets. She forced a smile and nodded her head. His watch beeped and he announced that his appointment had arrived and was in the boardroom. He kissed her cheek. Feeling very good about how he handled the situation, he said, "Good then we'll talk about it tonight." He put on his suit jacket that had been hanging from a coat rack near the door. On the way out of his office he said, "Baby, please don't forget the shirts."

Well at the very least, she had her answer. Nothing was going to change unless she regained some inner strength. The rape still hung over her like a weight of helplessness. It made her realize she had to find control and redefine what that was going to look like. Karen sat in her husband's chair looking over his large plush office. It was impressive. She wondered how differently he viewed this office. Jack, she was sure, saw power. That and prestige made his life happy. He was happy with his in-laws because Karen's parents adored him and saw the world through his same eyes. The three of them were pleased that everyone saw the family as the ideal and the beautiful success story.

# Addie

Addie blinked into the bathroom mirror. She turned her head-first right and then left. She nodded slightly in confirmation that she was healing quickly. A good application of makeup, long sleeves, and high collars would get her by at the studio. She was tired and bored with her sparse apartment. For her it was just a place to sleep. She never was a homebody and daytime television was a waste of time. She'd have her own show and change the face of daytime shows forever. Being the gofer at KTUC3 television station was going to be a short stop. *This time next year I'll be an anchor, and then watch me climb.* She already had a plan, and nothing was going to be an obstacle, certainly not the recent rape that she survived. *I have always taken care of myself, and that sadistic maniac got what he deserved!* The though actually empowered her.

Her thoughts of becoming a big celebrity had started at an early age. She could remember dressing up in her mother's clothes, applying her mother's makeup for hours at a time while her mother would leave her alone, from at the age of six.

Even at a young age she knew her many *uncles,* men that her mother spent time with, always put food on the table. She knew what her mom was. Her mom's hard life put years on a once beautiful face and that wasn't going to happen to Addie at any cost. Addie's face and body got her everything in life so far, and as long as there were men in the world who wanted her, she was going to have what she needed in life. She knew she was destined to be someone special. She was tall, blonde, and sexy. She walked with confidence and flare. Looking at herself in the mirror she thought, *There isn't a woman in the office that doesn't wish they looked like me.* She was already getting the attention from the important men in the office. *I'm in control of those men, not the other way around.*

Not all men were bad like her *uncles,* sexually abusing her when her mother was too drunk or exhausted to notice. Addie had actually fallen in love once. Unfortunately, he was a musician, a very poor musician. Poor was scarier than most things to Addie and as much as she loved David, love was just not enough. He had to be let go and she had to move on. She was far too driven to take care of any man. Other than David, the men in her life had to serve a purpose. They had to have something that she could profit from on her way up the ladder. Men owned the world and she took full advantage of her skills. If sleeping with some old, shriveled man got her what she needed, then so be it. Addie didn't need girlfriends; they were time-consuming and backstabbers. Being on her own was the way she liked it. Someday when she had it all, maybe then she would think about a man in her life. If that day ever came, even then the relationship would have to be on her terms.

The few hours spent in that garage last week were the most frightening of her life. That was one rape she wasn't sure she was going to survive. The others that took place as a child were painful, but she had taught herself to not fight back, it only made it more painful. She learned to transport her mind away from what they were doing to her body. She knew it would end and they would threaten her if she said anything to her mother. Then they would pretend it hadn't happened, until the next time. After she would feel dirty and embarrassed, and although she was a child, she knew she was something less than other girls.

This time as an adult she knew that man was going to kill her. Even as that terrifying thought was her reality at that moment, she realized she would rather be dead than be disfigured. If he took that away, it wouldn't be worth living. He would have taken all her power away. During the past week she spent little time going over the details of that night, it served no purpose. Her anger was spent, and her superiority over men was returned to her as she repeatedly plunged that knife into that animal. Her physical scars were no longer visible, it was time to move on. That horrible man was dead, her childhood lessons kicked in, once again her mind became detached from what he had done to her. That was just a brief interlude in her life. She dressed hurriedly, put on sunglasses to hide the fading bruises, and rushed out the door for the tanning salon. After all, she was supposed to have been in Aruba on vacation, not hiding in her apartment for a week healing.

She hated Tucson and couldn't wait to be an anchor on national television like ABC or FOX. She knew she had to be patient and jump through the hoops. She had to play the game but putting up with all the small-town politics was a pain.

## Ann

Ann sipped at her tea and stared into the fireplace. She had finally convinced Nicole she was okay to be left alone and that she should return to work. She couldn't believe how lucky she really was to have Nicky, the love of her life. It was hard to believe they have been together for twelve years now. Nicky had short cropped black hair that highlighted her heart shaped Asian face and delicate features. She was taller than Ann by two inches. She had an androgynous athletic build.

They had seen each other through some very rough times over that period. Somehow, their obstacles were always worked out together. Ann's memories were mostly about the good times and laughter they had shared with each other. These were the things Ann told herself to focus on when the nightmares of that night would creep back into her brain. The memories were all very disjointed when they invaded her as brutally as that psychopath had. Nicky would be awakened and gently rock Ann back to sleep, kissing Ann's tear-streaked face. Nicky had insisted she seek help with Ann's colleague, friend, and business partner, Kate Jordan. Kate and Ann had been best friends since middle school and were college roommates. They now had a successful psychiatric practice together here in Tucson. Kate and Nicky played on a women's soccer team together and the minute Kate had met Nicky, she knew Ann would fall hard for her. She introduced them and now she had two very best friends.

After her initial shock, the first priority for Nicky was to be assured that Ann's physical needs had been met. Ann had defiantly refused a rape kit, or to even call the police. Ann's volatile reaction to the suggestions told Nicky that Ann was hiding something more that took place that night. She reluctantly backed down and concentrated on Ann's contusions, cuts and bruises and relied on Kate to help heal Ann's deeper wounds. Being a surgeon, Nicky had seen many traumatized patients and knew when to back away. It was just as important to do so for this woman Nicky adored. She had faith that when Ann was ready, she would open up to her.

Ann wasn't ready to share all the details of that night with Nicky. She knew exactly where that garage was located, as soon as she looked back at it making her escape that night. It was in a secluded industrial park on the south side of Tucson on the route to Green Valley, not far from where she had been attending the seminar. She hadn't been truthful with Nicole, telling her she wasn't sure of the location of the garage and refusing to call the police. They had never kept secrets from each other before and Ann felt ashamed she was doing so now. She had a conflicting need to protect herself and the other two victims first. She needed time to work this out herself since this trauma had left her emotions and fears running through her head like a roller coaster.

It was too late for that poor butchered woman. The truth was, she didn't want anyone to be able to save that monster from bleeding out. Calling the police that night might have been the ethical and right thing to do, but she didn't care. There was not enough guilt to make her call the police. She didn't want the police sifting through the private evidence that *was her* and the other two women who survived the horror. The thought of that would be like a second violation. If his life had been saved, it would only have to put them through the trauma again with a trial. Who knows how they could live with the fear of waiting for that man to be released from prison, if he was even put there? The justice system was not foolproof and sometimes loopholes allowed these horrible people to go free on a technicality. The risk was too high. Even as she rationalized all this in her mind, her guilt at being an accomplice to a murder continued to torment her.

She waited this past week. Nothing had been reported on the news. She knew the identity of the butchered woman would help her family with their closure. That guilt won over her fear and she decided that she would drive by the garage to see if the premises had been secured off with yellow tape, before considering an anonymous call to the police.

Her heart started to race as she made the turn-off to the secluded road. Halfway down the block, she detected a lingering odor of smoke. As she approached the location of the garage, the smell got stronger. The garage had burned to the ground, and the area had not been cordoned off. Her stomach muscles tightened, and she felt faint for a second. Her hand gripped the steering wheel. *What happened?* She continued driving past the garage that now no longer existed. Her mind started to race. *Did one of the other two survivors come back and burn it to the ground?* Like herself, maybe one of the other women was also afraid for forensic evidence to be discovered?

She found herself parked in her office parking lot, not recalling the drive that had gotten her there. She was trying to wrap her head around the discovery of the burned warehouse that housed that madman's torture chamber. Finally, out of pure mental exhaustion, she stopped struggling with her thoughts and turned off the engine. Everything seemed to be a bigger more arduous effort since that night. Ann gave herself a few minutes to regroup and entered her office building. She was greeted by her receptionist. Although everything looked the same, Ann felt somehow out of place. It did not feel like her haven. She struggled trying to find normalcy. "Good morning, Dr Weiss. Welcome back. I was so sorry to hear about your accident."

Kate had told Peggy that Ann had been in a car accident. Ann said thank you to their receptionist and asked if Kate was in session. Peggy shook her head no, and Ann walked into Kate's office located just down the hall from her own.

Ann closed Kate's door and they both took seats on the couch. "Are you sure you are ready to come back to work tomorrow?"

Ann sighed and released the tension in her shoulders. "Frankly I'm a little concerned about concentrating on my patients, but I can't keep putting it off. A slight sob caught in her throat. She was surprised to know that there were actually any more tears left inside of her. She fought to control herself. Kate kicked into therapist mode, as she remained patiently silent, giving Ann time to continue. In that small space of time Ann and Kate realized that they both used that silent technique with their patients. She and Kate smiled at each other and laughed, breaking some of the tension. "Nicky doesn't quite understand the concept of personal distance between therapist and patient, meaning your best friend should not be your therapist. Even if she is you."

Kate chuckled. Her next comment took on a serious tone. "You know, Ann, seeing someone may not be a bad idea. Nicky and I are worried about you." She pressed a little harder. "I have a wonder woman I've recommended to some of my patients. She only works with abused and rape survivors."

Ann cut her off, not wanting to hear any more. "I will sort this all out and move on. I'm tired. I'm physically exhausted." With less certainly in her voice, "Most of all I'm really tired of him changing my life and turning my world upside down."

"Well, think about it. Annie, you know as well as I do that bastard has changed you forever. But the good news is you are on your way to stop being a victim. It's great you're angry. You are on schedule." Kate leaned forward and put her hand on Ann's knee. "You are okay, Ann, really you are. This horrible attack will give you firsthand empathy with your patients that have also survived a rape. They will be so lucky to have you. Use that to help them and yourself to work through this. Please know, I'm here for you always."

Ann knew she was very lucky to have Kate and Nicky in her life. The hugged, and

Ann sat back into Kate's comfortable couch. Ann wiped away the lingering tear. "The only doubt I have is self-doubt. That is an unfamiliar feeling for me. I need to deal with my trauma without throwing my training out the window." Ann stated emphatically, "And I will. Right now, I can't seem to talk to Nicky about this whole thing." Ann chuckled. "You know how clinical she is. She sees the world as black or white." With a smile on her face, Ann hit her fist into her other opened palm and imitated Nicky's voice. "Let's just fix the problem, next patient please."

Kate smiled at Ann's impersonation of Nicole. "That's why the two of you are so good together, you balance each other."

Suddenly and without preamble, Ann sighed deeply and confessed, "I drove by the place it happened. I told Nicky I didn't know where I had been taken." Ann shifted her position on the couch. "I knew she would take off at a racer's pace and call the police. I wasn't ready and I was too exhausted to fight her. She then proceeded to tell Kate about the burned down garage. For the next few minutes, they speculated at what could have happened. Their possible explanations did not seem plausible. Ann did not share with Kate that in the back of her mind she relived the blonde repeatedly stabbing that man. Ann shivered inside and could easily see that woman returning to burn down the warehouse.

# CHAPTER 2
## Four months later

Karen turned on the local KTUC 3 news at twenty minutes after the hour. Across town, Ann was watching as well. In their different locations, they both recognized Addie at the beginning of the weather forecast. She was the new weathergirl. After the initial shock of recognition, Karen almost expected to see her co-victim's face bruised and lip split, as she did that night. Now she knew the identity of *one* woman that was there that night. Ann too was startled upon learning who Addie was. An unsettling feeling overcame her, one she could not understand. Maybe it was the triggering of the memories that she was trying to bury. If they were to casually meet on the street, would they speak to each other, or merely speak to each other's knowing eyes? Would that chance meeting ever be played out with this woman or the other?

## Karen

Karen continued to try and convince herself that routine was getting back to normal. She kept busy with the boys, the country club, and now she had added marriage counseling to her schedule. Actually, marriage counseling turned out to be the wrong term. Jack did not attend sessions. He was much too busy and felt, since he was happy with their marriage, Karen was the one who needed to work things out.

Dr Martin was easy to talk to and he encouraged her to express her feelings freely. Unlike herself, she talked about how unhappy she was in their very first session. She had surprised herself that it had come out of her heart so easily. Still too uncomfortable enough to talk to him about the rape, she stuck to discussions he initiated. He asked her to share with him her best childhood memories. That was easy, it was her grandmother, "Meme", who had died when Karen was fifteen. Her parents were never present for her physically or emotionally. Meme lived in a small casita attached to their large villa in the foothills of the Catalina Mountains in Tucson. Karen would walk past the pool onto a short pathway that led to Meme's little house. The minute you opened her door, you would never know that this haven was just steps away from her parents' cold, massive house. Karen would rush home, drop her school bag in her room, and rush to the backyard. Before she would open the door to her grandmother's house, she would smell the freshly baked chocolate chip cookies waiting for her. Meme's house was cozy and decorated with two overstuffed chairs that enveloped you like a warm hug. Her little kitchen always welcomed you with a meal and its enticing aroma. Karen could not picture her mother growing up in Meme's house. They were so different. She had never met her grandfather; he died when she was six months old. She would stare at her grandparents' wedding picture over Meme's fireplace and feel the love and affection they had for each other. Her grandmother would smile and recall warm and funny stories about him. Karen ate her meals with Meme since her parents were rarely home. They were busy traveling or attending dinners to accept accolades for work they got others to do for community services.

Sometimes Karen and her grandmother would sit near the pool and Karen would share her day. There wasn't anything Karen couldn't share with her. Meme was sorely missed. Her brother Mathew was already in college at UCLA, but he loved Meme too. While she was still alive, he would try to get away from the dorm and classes to join them at his grandmother's little house for a long weekend. His few visits during the time Meme was alive, were some of Karen's best memories of the three of them together. She and her brother had been close as children and she always looked up to him. After Meme died, Karen would come home and cook for herself in Meme's kitchen. Many times, when her parents would travel, which was often, she would sleep in her grandmother's comfy soft bed. She would curl up with Meme's robe that still smelled of lilac, that smell of her grandmother. A few years later, Karen's heart was broken when her parents sold the house and moved into a condo. By then she was in college, but it left her with an emptiness that would never be filled.

During her second session, Karen talked a little bit about her parents. Her husband, Jack, and her dad had a lot in common. Kate's mother was very attractive. Both men had trophy wives, and both rarely were at home and involved with their families. Karen tried to remember her mother during those years. They too had a lot in common. Mom was always running to and from fundraisers, leaving quick instructions to the house staff. Her mother seemed happy enough throughout those years. Maybe that was just the way marriage was. Maybe she was just expecting too much. Maybe she and Jack were just like every other married couple. Then why was she so miserable?

Her head was still full of her thoughts from her earlier session, when she heard the front door close. A few minutes later, Jack was in the kitchen. He didn't acknowledge her presence and quickly sorted through the mail at the end of the kitchen counter. He seemed surprised when she asked about his day. She was determined to try making it more pleasant in the house for herself or at least for the boys. He stared at her a moment. She repeated her unfamiliar question to him. "Good. It was good." She waited for further conversation, of course, none was forthcoming. Karen continued to empty the dishwasher during the silence that followed. Jack left the kitchen and she heard his footsteps going upstairs. Well, so much for that attempt.

A tear slipped down her cheek. *"Thanks for asking,"* she said to herself. *"My day sucked."*

The following week she was looking forward to her morning appointment with Dr Martin. She was eager to explore with him her parents' mostly absent relationship with her and her brother, Mathew. Jack's relationship with his parents was similar. She didn't want that pattern to repeat itself for her boys. The appointment passed too quickly, and she sat in the car thinking about her session.

Her drive home took a sudden detour and she found herself parked at her mother's condo. Talking to her mother usually ended in frustration or hurt feelings, but maybe it was time to try and understand her parents' point of view. The housekeeper answered the door and welcomed her in saying her mother was due back within the hour. Karen decided to wait. Her session today had opened questions about her childhood she needed to explore with her mother. She wandered around the condo looking at the framed family photos. She and Jack looked so happy in their wedding picture. That was a day full of grand hopes for a beautiful future together. There were no pictures of her brother. Matthew lived in San Francisco with his lover, and her mother conveniently had no reminders of his existence on her artfully painted walls nor displayed on bookshelves. Karen really shouldn't be so judgmental since, sadly, she rarely spoke to him these days. Life just seemed to get in the way. It didn't help that Jack was uncomfortable with her brother being gay. Being busy with the boys was no excuse either. Just one more example of her taking the easier way out of uncomfortable situations.

The housekeeper announced that she was finished with her work and was leaving. They exchanged goodbyes and Karen went into the kitchen to make herself a cup of tea. She sat quietly at the kitchen table thinking about Matthew. They were close as children. They would play together for hours and rarely fought. Matthew was two years older than Karen and was very protective of her. He would read her stories and then they would act them out in the backyard to Meme's delight. They would occupy themselves happily in the absence of parents and other playmates. As they got older, Karen would rely on Matthew's opinion of the boys she found herself attracted to. He rarely found one that he approved of. He found one he approved of for himself, however, in his senior year of college. Actually, it was Karen who had met Greg the semester she met Jack and knew her brother would fall hard for Greg. He was Mathew's type: sensitive, funny and smart. It didn't hurt that he was very handsome in a college-preppy way. She was able to arrange a "chance meeting" at a coffee house near the college when Matthew was in town on break from UCLA. It only took a few weeks before the guys were flying back and forth from Los Angeles and Tucson. Mathew finally moved to California to be with Greg and they had been together ever since. Her brother's sexual orientation was known by both her parents but had never been acknowledged nor discussed. Karen sighed quietly as the kitchen clock ticked in the otherwise quiet house. *It was too bad for her parents. It was their loss.* Matthew and Greg were very happy and very devoted to each other. They had a relationship that Karen would give anything to have with Jack.

She heard her mother's keys being tossed onto the entry hall table. Her mother entered the kitchen and said, "I thought that was your car in the driveway." A bit suspiciously she asked, "What do I owe this honor of a visit?"

Karen suddenly wondered that herself. "Just out and thought I'd stop in." Her mother raised an eyebrow, waiting for more of an explanation since Kate's unannounced visits were not the norm. Karen dunked her tea bag a few times in her cup while she collected her thoughts. Thinking once again of Meme, she asked, "Mother, what are your fondest memories from your childhood?"

Her mother looked at her like she was from another planet. "Where did that come from?" Karen remained silent, not yet ready to share with her mother that she had started therapy. In her heart she knew her mother would see it as a weakness in her character. Her mother took a sparkling water from the refrigerator. She stood behind the counter and looked at her daughter seated across from her. "Karen, all I wanted as a child was to grow up and leave home. I know you loved your grandmother very much." That was said with a somewhat softer tone, only to be followed with, "My parents were very…" — she searched for the word — "unsophisticated. They had no ambition to better themselves." Her parents had always treated her grandmother as a mere inconvenience, but it hurt to hear how her mother described her beloved Meme. As an afterthought her mother added, "That's not what your father and I wanted for you and Mathew. We wanted to instill in both of you a wider view of world." She took a sip of her drink and continued, "So to answer your question, I don't have many good memories of my childhood, only boring ones."

Karen's view of her grandmother was anything but that. Defending Meme to her mother would only fall on deaf ears. Her fond memories were hers alone and she would keep them to herself to cherish. It was ironic to Karen that she and her mother's memories of their parents were virtually the same — unhappy. This short visit only confirmed what Karen already knew, she and her parents would never see the world the same way, and comfort or support was as dead here, in this house, as she got in her own with Jack.

## Addie

Grateful was not the word Addie felt when the weathergirl position became available. It was merely the next convenient step in her plan to move up the ladder to an anchor position and hopefully one in a major city. She had no qualms about undermining the other candidate who had better qualifications for the job. Addie had no experience in meteorology, but she knew how to play the game. From the minute she was hired at the studio, she zeroed in on the man in the Human Resources Department who makes the hiring decisions. He was married, which Addie knew was definitely to her advantage. She flirted with him every chance she got. From then on it was easy and finally she got him to sleep with her. She continued to make that relationship worth his time. The only thing that was becoming worrisome to her was that he was beginning to fall in love with her. That was not a complication she needed. When her opportunity presented itself, she had already set the groundwork. It was easy to convince him that reading a prompter didn't take a meteorologist degree. She tactfully pointed out to him that it wouldn't hurt the studio's ratings to have a much more attractive woman than the one leaving. Those arguments and a very special night at his favorite resort did the trick.

She was unfazed by the looks and snubs from the whole crew; they knew who she was, as did the whole office. That never bothered her in the past, nor did it now. *I know how to survive, and that is what life is all about.* She did her job and waited patiently. She already had that pre-pounce-butt-wiggle of a jaguar and knew just when to attack. Addie didn't have the time or the need to reflect on her past. Only losers felt sorry for themselves. She would never be a loser, that was the only promise her childhood had given her. Now she could concentrate on her next move without friendships or colleague interactions to get in her way.

## Ann

It was good to be back to work, it helped her to focus on someone other than herself. She was still experiencing nightmares but now they were becoming less intense. Nicky was always there to gently wake her and hold her close until she could fall back to sleep. Ann knew that Kate was right that she should get some counseling. She would make excuses that really sounded lame even to herself. Kate had recommended a specialist who only dealt with rape victims. She hated the thought of being called a victim. She wasn't ready to analyze her own motives for avoiding the issue, which included being afraid that if she were to fail to recover from this life changing trauma, how could she effective with her own patients? What would that say about herself as a psychiatrist? For now, she continued to avoid dealing with these fears and moved on.

Ann read over her notes taken last week about Meg. She was her next patient due in for her weekly appointment. Meg had been seeing Ann just a little over a year. It had taken her a number of months before she was able to open up and talk about her issues comfortably. Meg had younger twin brothers, Rick and Randy. She and Randy were always getting Rick out of bad situations at school. They were constantly coming to his rescue. Her mother made excuses for Rick's bad behavior, and then their father died when the boys were eleven; there was no discipline or consequences left for Rick. His teen years became intolerable. The summer he and his brother turned sixteen, the three kids went to the beach. Rick was swimming when he became exhausted and couldn't make it back to shore. He was drowning. He was within reach of Meg and Randy's help. They *chose* not to come to his rescue. They knowingly let him die. It was an instant solution that now, Meg, in her early thirties, was seeking help to release her demons.

Ann welcomed Meg in and closed the door while Meg took her seat on the couch. Small talk began about her week and slowly Ann turned the conversation around.

"Meg, last week we had to stop our session when we had just begun to talk a little about Rick's behaviors as a child. Could you tell me a little about what kind of trouble he would get into?"

Meg nodded and began. "Rick was always a bit peculiar even as a small child. He never had friends and I believe that other children sensed there was something not right about him. He didn't play with other kids. He would kick or bite them for no reason. He sometimes would just stare, like into empty skies." Meg hesitated as though she was aching to say something unspeakable. Ann remained silent and smiled at her reassuringly. Meg breathed in deeply, letting the air from her lungs out slowly. "He would hurt animals." Another pause and then she said, "I would find carcasses of cats and dogs under bushes in our backyard. They weren't even buried. Then he began collecting things like hair or fur and putting them in bottles." Meg's face saddened and she continued softly. "I started finding other containers in the closet with animal parts."

Ann remained quiet, waiting to see if Meg wished to continue. When she realized Meg didn't, Ann felt she would change up her next question to give Meg a chance to ease into what was obviously difficult for her. Ann stated, "That had to be difficult for you and Randy. Was Rick a sickly child?"

A little more relaxed Meg answered. "Yes, he was. He was pale and was always getting colds. My mother was having to stay home with him when he was sick. He wet the bed up until his early teens."

Ann needed to know the answer to the next question. It would tell her a lot about Meg's guilt for not saving her brother from drowning. "Meg, did Rick ever abuse you physically or sexually?"

Meg did not hesitate. Forcefully and unconvincingly stating, "No. He never hurt me or Randy."

Ann continued, "So, you and Randy didn't feel threatened by him? How about your mother?"

This is where Meg became visibly uncomfortable. "Occasionally he would throw things, but not *at us*. He once pushed my mother against the wall. Sometimes he would slap her when she tried to discipline him. The only times I felt weird around him …" — again, there was a hesitation — "he would sometimes hang around the bathroom door when I was showering. Once I saw him looking at me in my swimsuit and it made me uncomfortable." Defending him she continued, "But again, he was, you know, around thirteen and I guess that is normal for boys that age."

Ann quietly asked, "Did his twin make you uncomfortable at that age?"

Meg smiled at her, understanding why that questioned had been asked. "No, Randy never made me feel uncomfortable that way. I guess I'm still making excuses for Rick."

Ann was pleased that Meg was making the right connections to her past. "It's important for you to understand that defending Rick was a huge part of your childhood. Habits are hard to change." Their session ended for the day, and Ann felt good about Meg's progress. Next session she planned on easing into the real scary issue of letting her brother die.

Meg was her last patient for the day. As she began writing up her notes from Meg's session, she thought about her own trauma in that garage. Meg's brother had the classic signs of what she suspected was shared by the man that night she was attacked. She felt a sudden release of fear knowing he was dead. That was the moment she truly understood Meg's guilt because Ann shared it as well. She let that man die in that garage, and the burden of that was playing havoc in her day-to-day life.

Ann's own relationship with her brother couldn't have been more opposite. Michael brought a smile to her face. He was three years older than her. As kids, they would explore the forest behind their house for hours finding snakes, lizards and basically anything they could catch. They would pretend to be scientists taking notes and then letting the animals go. They would ride their bikes and build forts. Her parents let them sleep in the safety of their backyard in sleeping bags during summer break. They would tell each other made up scary stories. Ann occasionally found herself back in her bed in the house after one of Michael's imaginative narratives and accompanying scary voice. She and Michael were encouraged, nurtured, and well taken care of by loving parents. Ann had a wonderful childhood. Her parents were accepting and supportive of her when she came out at sixteen. Michael became a marine biologist and he loved traveling the world's oceans. Five years later, Ann and her parents' worlds were shattered when Michael was killed in an accident at sea. His body could not be recovered. There is an immense grief with the loss of any loved one. Finality and closure are much harder when there is no body to bury; no time to say goodbye. Still to this day, Ann sometimes expected him to walk through her door. Her mother died two years later, and her father remains broken and unreachable in his grief. He still lives alone in their house in Tahoe where Ann grew up. Occasionally she visited him. When she saw him, she saw an empty shell of himself. It was hard for her to accept as a psychiatrist she was unable to help him.

# CHAPTER 3
## Karen

The country club board induction banquet was tomorrow night. She was dreading it. Since the attack, she was fearful of going out at night. She was finding it more difficult going out to the country club for weeks now. It didn't help that the country club was where she had been abducted. Her father was being honored at the dinner, so she didn't have a choice. Jack was also looking forward to going. He had a chance at procuring a highly sought-after client for his law firm, who was attending the affair; that would be a big feather in his cap.

She was checking over her outfit for the event when the boys ran into the bedroom. Jack Jr. jumped up on the bed followed by his younger brother, Mark. They rolled around wrestling and sending pillows onto the carpet. Karen rolled her eyes at their antics. She attempted to put on a stern face. "Boys, you guys know better. Now stop." They weren't fooled one bit. She sat on the bed and ruffled their sandy blonde hair. She adored them. Jack Jr. was referred to as JJ. He was twelve and their athlete. He was also the spitting image of his handsome father. Mark was ten and the quieter, more thoughtful, sensitive one. He was blessed with incredible sky-blue eyes. She kissed each boy on the forehead. "What do you say we order pizza tonight?" She was very careful to make sure they ate healthy and she knew they would jump at the chance for pizza. She got the reaction she wanted. They both shouted their approval and started rolling around on her bed again. This time she joined them, laughing and tickling each other.

The boys took their rambunctious selves to the backyard to play while waiting for the pizza to arrive. Karen took a beer from the refrigerator and turned on the news. She leaned against the counter and took a sip. Since Karen had learned Addie's identity, she made a point to watch the weather report. It was almost an obsession. She would stare at her every expression on the television, looking for a hint of what was going on in Addie's head since that horrible night. Of course, she rationally knew she would never see what she was looking for. She wondered about the other woman too, the one who grabbed him by the hair. Wherever she was, Karen was thankful for her bravery and hoped she was doing okay. The memory of that sent a shiver down her spine. Lately she wondered a lot about both women; it reminded her she was not alone. She had her boys, and was so grateful for that, but otherwise she felt alone.

Jack was going to be working late tonight, again. She suspected he really was with another woman, but at this juncture of their marriage, she no longer really cared. Her therapy had little to do with her marriage.

That was okay, too, because she was starting to learn a lot about herself. As she thought about these things, she also knew that as much as she didn't want to take the boys away from Jack, she had to have more respect for herself. She didn't feel strong enough yet to leave him. The boys loved their dad. Taking the boys and leaving Jack would be hard enough, but then there were her parents and in-laws that thought Jack walked on water. All that was for their own appearances, and she didn't want to be a part of that any longer either. How do you just leave everything you were *expected* to be and walk away from family? She just hoped she would continue to find her inner strength, which had been severely damaged by the rape. When the time was right, she would venture out on her own.

Jack's parents lived up in Scottsdale. They had a huge house just for the two of them. Jack's younger sister, Susan, lived close by her parents, also in Scottsdale, with her husband, Mike, and Jack's two nieces. Karen liked Susan. She was down to earth and didn't find the need to put on airs. Karen's boys were a few years older than their cousins and they really had little in common, so they didn't see each other much. Karen's in-laws were going to be watching the boys over the weekend. The banquet dinner tonight was the first of the busy country club's planned activities for the next two days.

Karen had packed the boys a suitcase. She put them in the car and attached their bikes to the bike rack. They had their snacks for the two-hour drive, and each had their electronic devices in the back seat with them. They were off.

Karen pulled into the large circular driveway and was met at the car. It was her mother-in-law's maid, Maria, with a big happy grin. "Hello, Mrs Michaels. So nice to see you."

"Good to see you too, Maria. How is your family? Your handsome son, how is he doing?"

Maria's face lit up. "He is wonderful, am so proud of him. He will be starting his first year at Arizona State."

"My goodness, already? It's hard to believe. The last time I saw him he was in middle school."

Susan came out of the house just then and helped Karen remove the boy's bikes from the rack while Maria and the boys went inside. Susan was slim, tanned, and healthy looking. She always seemed happy and content. Kate recognized she was a little jealous. *Maybe I just married the wrong brother.*

"I am looking forward to taking the boys biking. They enjoyed the trail I found for us the last time they were up camping. The boys were disappointed, Jack couldn't stay and Mike's parents were out of town. Mike and I enjoyed being with the kids. We had fun."

Karen remained silent. Jack had again lied to her. The last time the boys were here was in October. She knew exactly when it was. It was the night she had been attacked. Jack had said he and his father were taking the boys camping for a few days. It was *after* Jack begged her to forgive him for the affair and promised it would never happen again.

Karen forced a smile and said, "Right. I don't remember where Jack had to go?"

Susan closed the latch on the bike rack and Karen followed her up the drive with the second bike. "Flagstaff. I remember he had snow gear in the car. He left us the name and number of the lodge up there."

She calmed her building outrage. "Of course, now I remember." Karen felt betrayed and angry. He not only lied that it was over, he continued seeing whoever she was. Jack's late nights only confirmed her suspicions were right. He had told her he had fired the woman. Maybe he did or maybe he didn't, or maybe it was just another woman now.

Those and other questions cluttered Karen's mind as she returned to Tucson to get ready for the banquet. She found Jack in the shower, having returned from his golf game. That was if he really was playing golf. He came into their bedroom and gave her a passing peck on her cheek. "Better get a move on. I don't want to be late picking up your parents."

The women were dressed in their finest. Diamond necklaces and rings competed with the crystal chandeliers for the reflective light. The men were in their tuxedos pulling at their uncomfortable bow ties and cummerbunds. Jack found their seats at the front table where her father was to be honored. Jack pulled out her mother's chair for her and as an afterthought Karen's chair. The present board president tapped his champagne glass with his spoon and the crowd silenced. He welcomed everyone and announced dinner was about to be served.

Karen and her mother sipped at their wine quietly while her father gave Jack advice about how to approach his prospective client her father had arranged for Jack to casually meet. This or similar business was always the discussion at family dinners. Karen wondered if her mother was as bored as she was. During lulls in the conversation, Karen was acutely aware of Jack's furtive glances at the women at the next table. They were definitely enjoying their flirting. Her parents seemed to be oblivious to the woman seated next to them keeping Jack's attention or vice versa. Her father just droned on about some case law.

Jack didn't even have the decency not to flirt with someone right in front of her. Karen excused herself to go to the lady's room. Her mother looked up at her and said, "Don't be long, the ceremony is about to begin."

Karen took a seat in the lady's lounge. There were golf and tennis matches, and a dance scheduled for the following two days. She knew she just couldn't do it. She sat there thinking how she was going to get out of attending. It was all so exhausting. The stress of the last few months sat on Karen's shoulders like a heavy weight. Her life had become overwhelming and out of control. A woman appeared in front of her. She had lost track of time. It was her mother. She discreetly leaned over Karen. Quietly as not to draw attention to another woman who had just entered the lounge, she said, "You have five minutes to get back to the table. I don't know what your problem is, but *do not* embarrass your father and husband." She turned and exited.

She took a few more moments to center herself. She checked her hair in the mirror and could see the darkening skin under her eyes where lately more makeup needed to be applied. She had not been sleeping well and it was beginning to show on her face.

Karen returned to the table and somehow got through the rest of the evening. She smiled and graciously accepted congratulations on her father's appointment and made small talk. Finally, the night was over and the four of them left. Jack and her father continued talking in the car on the way to her parents' house. Jack pulled into her parents' driveway only to discover her dad wanted them to come in so that he and Jack could finish their discussion. Karen couldn't even give the excuse that she had to get back to the boys.

The men went into her father's study, she and her mother into the family room. Her mother removed and placed her jewelry on the bar and made herself a drink. She waved a vodka bottle toward Karen. "Want one?" Karen shook her head no. Her mother took her seat across from Karen.

Karen came right to the point. "Jack has been having an affair or affairs for some time now. At least a year."

Her mother never changed her expression and took a sip of her drink. After what seemed to be too long of a pause, she said, "Jack is a handsome and successful man. Women throw themselves at men like that."

Karen waited for her mother to continue. No further *wisdom* was forthcoming. Her mother just sat there looking at her. Annoyed, Karen asked, "So that's that? Jack isn't responsible for his affairs?"

Her mother put her drink down on the side table and casually clasped her hands in her lap. "You are intelligent and worldly, your father and I made sure of that. You are a beautiful, lovely woman." She crossed her legs and leaned back into her chair. "You have a lovely home and handsome children. Many people would be very envious of your life."

Karen was livid at her mother's complacency. No, it was more than that, she was enraged. As calmly as possible, Karen asked, "Just to be sure I'm understanding you, you too have a privileged life and handsome husband. It would be fine with you if Daddy had affairs?" Her mother's silence and stoic face was more than silence, it was her mother's confirmation. Apparently, her father's station in life also earned him the right to have affairs. She sat there dumbstruck. The coldness, her parent's constant absence from her and Mathew's lives, and now the knowledge that her father had or continues to have affairs. She felt hollow inside. She had nothing meaningful, other than her boys, in her life.

Jack and her father entered the room. Jack had his dinner jacket over his arm. "Ready to go home."

Karen suddenly realized that she had *never* really had a home.

# Two Weeks Later
# Ann

Kate locked her office door and joined Ann in the lobby. They both said goodbye to their receptionist, Peggy, and headed to the restaurant. It was time for their weekly business lunch meeting, and they looked forward to it and getting out of the office. Their favorite Mexican restaurant was just around the corner and there was no reason to drive. They walked in and were met by Rubin, the waiter who always saved them a table in the back so they could spread out their expense sheets.

Ann was a creature of habit and always ordered the same dish for lunch. Kate picked up the menu and chose one from her three favorites. Rubin had their margaritas ready and placed them on the table.

They made short work of covering the office responsibilities and orders for supplies. Kate smiled shyly. "You'll be proud of me. I met this guy and I'm thinking about going out with him."

Ann raised her eyebrows in mock surprise. "Really? Only thinking about it?"

Kate chuckled. "Okay, so I'm going out with him this weekend. He might even know Nicky. He works at Tucson Medical Center."

Ann teasingly said, "Well, maybe we will keep growing our little family."

Kate held up her hands, palms facing Ann. "Hold up. I *haven't* even gone out with him yet. By the way, when was the last time you had some time together with Nicky?"

"Why do you ask? Did she say something?"

The tone in Kate's voice turned serious. "Ann, she's concerned. She feels like you aren't sharing your feelings with her since the attack."

Ann's guilt was written on her face. "I'm aware I have been avoiding the subject. Kate, she is the most ethical person I know. I took part in letting that man die."

Kate reached across the table and took Ann's hand in hers. "So, I take it you haven't shared *all* the details of that night with her?" Ann silence confirmed her assumption. "She knows you better than anyone else. She needs to know how you are struggling. She feels like you are pushing her away and it scares her. She won't judge you any more than I do. You have always trusted each other. Trust her now."

Ann nodded in agreement, although her face showed her nervousness. "I will, I will tell her."

Nicky got home early after making her afternoon patient rounds. She found Ann in the kitchen prepping for their dinner. "Hi, baby."

Ann looked up into Nicky's beautiful face and smiled. "Hi yourself."

Nicky came around the counter and took Ann into her arms. They exchanged a long and lingering kiss. She then took a cold beer from the refrigerator and popped the tab.

Ann returned to putting dinner together, and asked, "How was your day?"

"Good. I had two surgeries this morning that went really well and a consultation with a new patient with an interesting case." She took a big gulp of her beer and burped. "How was your day?"

Ann laughed. She pulled Nicole back into her arms. "Come here and don't burp into my face." They kissed again. "I'm all prepped and about to start dinner. Go relax." *Go relax* was more of an order than a comment. Relaxing was something Nicky had a difficult time with.

Nichole Chen had been raised in a structured Chinese home that consisted of school, study, more studying, and very high expectations. Grades and education were the only things that her parents believed in for her and her sister. There was no time for anything else. Nicky's sister, Michelle, became an accomplished musician and Nicky became an accomplished surgeon. There would be no other options once their parents set them on their appointed goals. Their parents were very proud of their daughters. All that pride for Nicky suddenly was withdrawn when she came out. All the perfect grades and accomplishments were suddenly forgotten, and shame took their place.

Her sister was Nicole's only family support and her career had taken her to New York. The sisters tried to visit each other at least twice a year and only when her parents weren't visiting Michelle in New York. Nicky's parents still lived in Tucson maybe two miles from them. It was Michelle, Nicky's sister, who checked in on them from New York.

Nicky went into the adjoining family room with her beer and turned on the news. She sat down in the easy chair. A few minutes later, she said, "Wow, looks like that weather girl at KTUC3 was murdered." Ann instantly jerked her head up to look at the television, which was visible from the kitchen. There on the screen was a picture of Addie with her straight white teeth, and weather girl smile.

Ann entered the living room and stood staring at the television in disbelief. She and Nicky listened to the reporter state that her body had been found in her apartment this morning when she failed to report for work. She had been repeatedly stabbed and beaten to death. There were no further details and no suspects at this time. The next footage was a live picture outside Addie's apartment showing yellow tape around the building and police officials coming in and out of the entrance.

Ann's legs started to shake. It had been six months since Ann's attack. Ann knew nothing about Addie, who she was, or her hopes and dreams. Yet, they had shared the most intimate and frightening moment of their lives together. The thought accompanied a physical ache to her chest. She sat down on the arm of Nicky's chair. The reporter continued, "Ms Carson's mother, her only known surviving family member, has been notified and she is on her way to Tucson. There will be a private burial. This tragedy has left the station and our Tucson community shaken and we hope a suspect will soon be apprehended." The reporter then went on to another story.

Ann reached across Nicky for the remote on the end table and turned off the television. With a catch in her voice she said, "That was one of the women in the garage that night. A wide-eyed, silent "wow" crossed Nicole's face as she saw the tension and sadness on Ann's face. She pulled Ann into her lap, letting her sob and holding her until Ann's shaking subsided.

All the details of that night poured out of Ann with fear, anger, sorrow, and ending with the guilt of how she had left the man to die. She also shared that she had returned to the garage the following week to discover it had been burnt to the ground. "I can't believe she had survived that night only to be murdered by someone else. I'm sorry I didn't tell you all this from the beginning. I have been struggling with the guilt of leaving him there to die, instead of calling the police. I was afraid to tell you."

Nicole wiped the remaining tears from Ann's face. "Afraid! Oh no, honey, I understand. When rape victims come into the hospital, I see the result of what that kind of violence can do. Visible violence that is so hard to believe both physical and mental. I saw you battered and bruised, and I felt helpless to only be able to take care of the physical pain. I am so grateful to Kate. She has reminded me to be patient with you."

Ann smoothed down Nicky's shiny black hair. "God, baby, you have been."

"Annie, I could never judge you. Our instincts are to save lives. That is what we both do for a living. I am not sure what I would have done if it had been me."

Ann savored the release she felt. She had caused the woman she so loved both pain and anxiety. Her job would be a lot easier if her patients opened up to her sooner.

It became painfully clear to Ann why it was sometimes hard to do that, even in a safe environment.

Ann explained her feelings for the need to protect herself and the other two women by not calling the police. For that, she didn't regret leaving him to die in that garage. Calling the police would only cause them repeated trauma with rape kits, exams, and a million questions they did not want to share and relive. There was no reason to put them through it again. She did regret that the remains of the fourth woman's identity may never be known due to the fire. They continued to talk and speculate about who might have set the fire. Ann's gut feeling was it had been Addie. Her memory of Addie's detachment as she stabbed him over and over left a vivid picture in Ann's mind. It was not hard to believe that Addie could have returned to watch the man take his last breath before setting the building on fire. Addie's reaction had been a primeval rage that night.

Ann felt a huge weight had been lifted from her chest, having finally shared everything with Nicky. She went into their bedroom to shower. A few minutes later Nicky stepped into the shower with her. The smile on Nicky's face and the soapy hand that caressed her breasts told Ann that she had been forgiven for holding back the details of that October night, and that they were about to start another, more enjoyable, release tonight.

## Karen

Karen too began following Addie's murder story on the nightly news, as well as in the newspaper. It was a diversion from her thoughts about the night of the banquet and her discussion with her mother. She had skipped her last two sessions with Dr Martin. She was ashamed to share her present life circumstances with him. She had only shared her childhood memories with him so far. If she were to open up to him, in her heart, she knew he would judge her for not leaving Jack. That wouldn't be fair because he couldn't possibly understand that leaving Jack was not that simple. For whatever reason, the boys adored their father, which was a total mystery to her, since Jack rarely found time to be with them. She knew she was also putting off dealing with the rape. She was not at all comfortable doing that kind of therapy with a man. For now, she would try and sort things out herself.

The other night Jack actually had the nerve to initiate sex with her. She stopped him immediately and told him she wasn't, and never would be, his second choice. She said to him bluntly that she knew he was sleeping around. He didn't even try to deny it, and as usual, there was no discussion that followed. He just started not coming home most nights. That was fine too. She no longer felt any attraction to him and wouldn't have to worry about him giving her an STD. She wondered if her mother ever thought about that. Maybe her parents no longer had sex either. *This is all so fucking depressing!* After her last session with Dr Martin, she had been thinking more about Mathew. She felt badly that they didn't keep in touch for little more than Christmas and birthday cards. She felt so isolated and unsupported by her parents, maybe it was time to touch base with her brother.

Karen was beginning to enjoy Jack being out of the house more. There was a sense of freedom making day to day decisions without his involvement. If, as her mother suggested, his infidelity was her price to pay for her *good life,* for now, so be it. She wanted a divorce but knew she was not yet ready to go against both Jack and her parents. The three of them would be humiliated and would support each other in any way they could to prevent a scandal. She would have to bide her time, get a job and start earning money on her own, because Jack would definitely fight for custody of the boys just to say he did. Only when she was self-sufficient would she file for divorce. For now, she would have to hide from Jack any job she could get. He would become suspicious and file before she was unable to support herself and the boys, and they would be taken from her. She had to be smart and prepared for going it alone. One step at a time. A job being number one.

She was thankful she had gotten her MBA, although she had never used it. It should be easy enough to explain on a cover letter that she was waiting until her kids were both in school before going to work. That sounded plausible. She could highlight all her charity work and country club organizational skills on her resume. Her next concern would be hiding a full-time job from Jack while balancing the boys' schedule and social responsibilities. She was motivated and she would make it happen. Other women handled it, all except keeping their job a secret from their husbands. *No matter, I will find a way.* It also helped that she took care of the household budget. Now she would designate a monthly amount to go directly into a private bank account for herself. That should have happened a long time ago. Live and learn.

She was really excited about her plan and could see herself getting an apartment set up for herself and the boys before filing for the divorce. With some work experience under her belt eventually she could even move out of state away from Jack and her parents. Why not? After the divorce it would be harder staying in town and being around them. Once again Mathew came to mind, and she totally understood his need to leave.

She picked up the boys from school and stopped on the way home at the supermarket. The boys did their homework while she made dinner. It was a surprise when Jack walked in. He didn't look happy and he hadn't come home for dinner in over a week. Mark excitedly ran to him with big hugs. He smiled and hugged both boys. JJ was the first to speak. "Hey, Dad, are you staying home tonight?" Jack had explained his nights away to the boys as business trips. Jack didn't take business trips.

"Yes, JJ. I won't be traveling so much."

Karen's heart sank. His newest affair must have ended. That was going to complicate her life. He would be around the house more and she didn't want him to become suspicious of her plans. She addressed Jack and the boys in a pleasant voice, she needed Jack to think everything was normal at home. "Why don't you guys wash up for dinner." The boys ran off racing each other to the bathroom.

As if this was their everyday routine, Jack gave her one of his charming business smiles. "What's for dinner?"

Karen tried to keep the mood light. "Well, first you'd better wash your hands too." Jack searched her face for a more hidden meaning. He only saw an innocent smile on her face.

He came into the kitchen and stood next to her at the sink and washed his hands, drying them on her kitchen towel. "After the boys finish their homework, I'll throw the ball around with them in the backyard."

She patted him on his shoulder, that being the only physical contact between them in weeks. Free of any sarcasm, she said, "I'm sure the boys would love that."

They sat down as a family and started eating their dinner. The boys were obviously glad to see their dad and chattered away, telling him all the things that they were doing at school. Jack asked lots of questions.

After dinner, Jack and the boys went out to the yard while Karen cleared the table and cleaned up the kitchen. She watched them through the kitchen window. They were tossing the ball and were thrilled to have their dad's attention. Karen started to feel a little guilty about her plans to take the boys from him. She was also feeling less confident than she did two hours ago. She forced her thoughts back to her present situation and knew being on her own was the right decision.

They watched a Disney movie with the boys and after their showers, they pleaded for an extra hour, which was denied because they had school in the morning. Karen went into her bedroom, got in her night gown, and climbed under the covers to check out new movies on HBO. She assumed Jack was working and would continue to sleep on the couch in his office, instead he entered the bedroom and, fully clothed, laid down beside her. Karen wondered what was going on in his mind and continued to silently surf the menus of films titles.

Jack cleared his throat nervously. "I was thinking of maybe going to one of those marriage counseling sessions with you." She hadn't had any need to tell him she had stopped seeing Dr Martin and just waited for him to continue. "You know, I have just been so swamped at work lately." *That and screwing* she thought. He continued, "You know I love you, Karen. I agree we just have been neglecting each other lately." He waited to hear her say she loved him too. Karen couldn't bring herself to say those empty words he wanted to hear. She said nothing. He tried another tactic. "I want you to be happy."

Karen saw an opportunity and jumped at it. "I think part of me being unhappy has to do with not feeling fulfilled. You have a career that is challenging. Don't get me wrong, I love being here for the boys—" She thought it would sound better if she added, "And you, but now that they are both busy with school and friends, my country club activities aren't enough. You know what I'm saying?"

Jack took the bait. "Yes, I definitely get it. I think getting a part-time job would be nice for you. I just don't want it to interrupt or interfere with the boy's schedule and our family time."

Karen was pissed. *What family time? Time for you to find your next affair. How dare he!* She suppressed her anger, not wanting to shut down the discussion. As calmly as possible, she stated, "We are lucky to be in a position to hire an au pair. I think it would be great if the boys could learn another language and we both could relax knowing there would always be someone here for the boys if we get stuck at work, or whatever." She was convinced that Jack would see that as a great idea. His social status was always the most important part of their lives in his eyes. Karen thought she could actually see his eyes shining brighter. She could see him already taking the idea as his own and impressing his parents and in-laws.

Karen smiled to herself. *I'm sure he is already planning what the au pair should look like and how long it would take to get her into bed.* Karen could care less. She could watch his enthusiasm build. "Honey, I think that would be a great solution. Yes, that is a good idea. I'll start interviewing right away."

*I bet you will.* Karen didn't want him to take over leaving her out of it and making the wrong choice for the boys. In a little stronger voice, she said, "Jack, I do want some say in who we hire."

"Of course, honey, of course."

She knew she had to flatter him in some way, ending the discussion on a good note and making him feel she still depended on him. "Maybe you could also help me put together a resume?"

That obviously puffed out his chest. He nodded, assuming she should ask for his expertise. "I would be happy to."

Nothing more was mentioned about marriage counseling. That was fine with Karen. She had no intention of saving this marriage.

# CHAPTER 4
## Ann

Ann had not yet arrived at the office. Kate opened the office early, hoping to catch up on a few things before her first patient of the day. The office was quiet, and she got right to work. Her mind occasionally wandered to her date with Brad. A smile came to her face. The date went well. He was smart, funny, and best of all a good listener. It didn't hurt that she found him very attractive as well.

Kate had been nervous about starting to date again after a long relationship that ended badly. She had stayed in the relationship much longer than she should have. She was convinced he would want to settle down and get serious about working on their relationship. Travis would try for a while and then lapse back into his comfort zone, which was complacency. He never really listened, which was frustrating to her. She would be talking to him a good two minutes when he would be distracted by the game on the television or simply walk out of the room with his phone. It was infuriating. It always made her feel invisible. It was over three years into their dating when Kate discovered the cause of his constant distractions. Unknown to her, he had a gambling habit. That was the only thing that constantly occupied his mind. He had a great job and made good money. Only when he asked her for a large amount of money did she learn he was in deep trouble.

He was in a total panic when she said no to his request for money. She told him he needed to see someone about his addiction. There was a nasty exchange of words, and he walked out the door and that was the end of the relationship. She heard from a mutual friend a few months later that he had lost his job and had started drinking heavily. Then he moved out of state. The relationship ended so abruptly that it shook her confidence, not only in her choice of a partner, but as a psychiatrist who didn't recognize the signs of his addiction. Ann and Nicky had been there to help pick up the pieces.

Kate heard their receptionist coming in and greeted her. Ann arrived on time a few minutes later. Ann started her day by making coffee for the office. She poured herself a cup and one for Kate, bringing it to her and placing it in front of her on the desk. She said, "How was your date with Brad?"

Kate took a sip of her coffee. "Good. I like him and we enjoyed each other's company." Her lips puckered and Ann recognized that gesture was Kate's way of questioning herself and waited. Finally, she said, "I just don't want to move too fast."

Knowing Kate's history with Travis, she said, "I get that. So, I guess that means there will be a second date?"

Kate smiled and blushed slightly. "Yes. He's handsome and he smells good too."

Ann's smile turned into a wide grin. "I give you maybe two more dates and then Nicky and I have to meet and approve of him."

"Yes, Mother." Redirecting the subject matter, she asked, "So, how is your love life these days?"

Ann thought about last night's love making with Nicky. Nicky had made love to her slowly and sensually. Earlier in the evening she had told Nicky everything about that traumatic night. Her mind felt release and Nicky made her body release like only Nicky could.

"Nicky smells good too." Kate laughed. Ann took a seat and her tone turned more serious. "I told her about that night and why I made the choices I did. You were right. There was no judgment, only support. I'm so lucky to have you both in my life."

"We both love you, Ann, and want to be there for you. You guys have always been there for me."

Kate's statement, along with finally opening up to Nicky, warmed her heart and it was the first time in weeks that she felt her confidence returning. This attack had shaken her so badly and she had been reluctant to even speak of it to Nicky until last night. "One more thing. That weather girl, Addie, all over the news, was one of the women that was beaten and raped too." Kate looked visibly shaken. With her hand over her mouth, she gasped. Ann continued, "I told Nicky that I think she was the one who burned that warehouse down. Her violence when she killed that man was very scary. It is so sad to me that she had to die violently as well, after surviving that night."

Kate finally found her shaken voice. "Annie, how horrible. The irony of escaping death only to be killed later by another person is just so sad."

Ann closed her eyes and nodded. "I know I can't get her out of my mind. That poor woman. She was attacked a second time. She had to live that terror all over again." Ann shuddered at the memory. She continued with, "I hope the person who did this is caught soon."

In the weeks that followed, the story of Addie's murder and all the speculation began to unfold. Employees from the station began to be interviewed. Addie's co-workers did not paint a pleasant picture of her. The rumors about the affair started to surface. It was discovered that Addie had more than just one affair at the office. Now theories of jealously and betrayal came into play. Two different men became suspects. It was an ongoing story that kept it the lead story nightly for weeks before the leads fell through and less was reported. A few months later it all seemed to become old news with almost no mention and replaced by fresh stories of sensational news. The mystery of Addie and her life seemed to vanish with her death, except for Ann and Karen.

# Karen

Jack didn't press his luck and slept on the couch in the office. He had left before Karen and the boys were up. Karen didn't want to ruin the progress she had made last night, but she certainly wasn't going to have him back in her bed. She was relieved that he had left the bedroom last night after their discussion. She showered and got the boys ready for school. She drove back from dropping them off, which had become the norm since Jack had not been around to do so much. She headed into the home office to work on a resume. It looked like Jack had started one for her. It was obvious, although she had little work experience, he had no knowledge of any talents she had brought to the country club. She started listing fundraising, organizing charity events. She realized she had interviewed and took bids from vendors and overseen their work. The list of her skills started to grow and with it her excitement. This had all been volunteer work but with her MBA, it was going to get her a paying job. It was going to secure her freedom.

Yesterday she had left a message on Mathew's phone. As she began to compose her cover letter, she saw his name come up on her phone. She stopped what she was doing and quickly answered his call. "Hi there, I see you got my message."

"Yes, it was a nice surprise." Mathew's voice sounded pleased. He then sounded a little concerned. "Is everything all right?"

Karen could hear the tone of his voice change. "Yes, yes of course," she said reassuringly. "It's just been so long. I wanted to see how you and Greg are doing."

"Good. We are busy but finding time to enjoy San Francisco. It's a great town and there is plenty to do. It was a good decision for us to move up here. Greg loves his job working at the *San Francisco Chronicle*. He has his own column now."

Karen heard the pride in her brother's voice. It made her smile. "And you? What are you up to these days?"

"It worked out well when Greg got this opportunity. I just transferred from the Los Angeles office with the firm to here."

Mathew was a financial advisor and Karen was very proud of him for standing up for himself when their father was furious that he dropped out of law school. "That sounds like it all worked out pretty smoothly."

"It did. So, tell me how you guys are doing?"

Karen hadn't shared much with her brother in some time. It was not the time to catch him up to speed with her present situation, certainly not over the phone. "So much to catch up on. We really need to see each other; it's been way too long."

Mathew was not comfortable around Jack and always felt his disapproval. Mathew wasn't sure if Jack was homophobic or just once again had to be on the same page as Mathew's parents with their judgments. Jack needed his in-law's approval even more than Jack's own parents. For whatever reason, Jack would never receive approval from his own parents, Mathew didn't care to know why. Mathew had felt replaced by Jack in his parents' eyes, and Jack ate it up and loved to flaunt it in his face. Visiting his sister in Tucson would be awkward for everyone. "You know you're definitely right. What about you and the boys coming up for a visit?"

Karen really wanted to spend time with him to reconnect. "I would love that. The boys are still in school, and to tell you the truth, getting away alone sounds really good. I could use the break from the boys for a few days. Let me know when it would be convenient time for your schedules."

They spoke a few more minutes while Mathew checked his calendar and it was decided the following weekend sounded good. She would get a flight out on Friday afternoon.

Karen knew when Jack got home, he would not be thrilled to hear that she was going to visit the *black sheep of the family*. He probably felt it was an inconvenience for him to pick up the boys from school on Friday and then have to entertain them all weekend while she was gone. He didn't say so, but it was written all over his face. She really didn't care that he was only keeping silent to keep the peace now that things were going his way again.

## Ann

Ann sensed there was something more going on with Meg than she was willing to share. Ann sensed that her demeanor was different when she walked into her office for their weekly appointment. Meg took her seat on the couch and started fidgeting with the strap on her shoulder bag. Her tension was apparent as she was the first to speak. "Dr Weise, I think I'd like to ask you a question." Ann smiled and nodded for her to continue. Meg repositioned herself on the couch nervously. "Do you think I'm a bad or sick person for letting my brother die?"

Meg had never directly asked Ann that type of a question before, Ann knew she must not hesitate. She did not want Meg to feel that she was analyzing her response. With a firm voice she said, "No. I do not. Meg, you and your brother Randy were caring a heavy burden all through your childhood. Keeping your brother out of trouble was not a responsibly that you as children should have had to undertake." As a therapist, Ann knew it was inappropriate. It was unprofessional to talk about personal experiences with a patient. It was hard not to be able to share with Meg that she too struggled with that very issue. She too had let someone die. It didn't matter that he had been a deranged stranger. "Let's talk a little more about that burden. Did you and your brother feel the need to protect the knowledge of Rick's behavior from your mother?"

Being reassured of her mental health, Meg relaxed a little. "Yes. We still do, because we talk about it. He feels more strongly about it than I do. She shouldn't know about the horrible things he does."

Ann was very aware of the present tense, *does. Perhaps a slip of tenses.* Casually she asked her, "Is your mother still alive?"

Meg nodded. "Yes. She is in assisted living here in Tucson. She really is too young to be there, but her physical health now is pretty fragile."

Ann remembered Meg only briefly talking about her mother. "I see. I'm sorry to hear that. Tell me more about your mother's relationship with you and your brothers."

Meg took a moment to focus on where to start. She began, "My mother did not have an easy life. She grew up in a very religious family. Her father saw everything as a sin. She left her father, who was quick to use a strap for any minor offences, for a marriage of abuse from my father." A flash of visible disgust crossed her face before continuing. "My father was a harsh and brutal man. Every time Rick would get into trouble, my father would beat him and then my mother as well for not raising him properly." To clarify, Meg explained. "My father was a truck driver and most of the time he was on the road." She stopped, seemingly lost back to those times.

Ann gently prodded, "Did your father beat you and Randy as well?"

She said a little evasively, "Not so much. We stayed away as much as we could when he was home. Occasionally, he would slap us around but nothing like what my mom and Rick got. Rick baited him. It was like he was asking for a beating. It was not fair because my mom had to suffer too."

"I recall you mentioned in an earlier session that Rick sometimes would push your mother around for any minor offense. How would she respond to that abuse?"

"He usually listened to me telling him to stop. Actually, those were the only times I would see Rick cry. He never apologized to Mom, but you could see he was sorry."

Ann was getting a much clearer picture of Rick's psychosis. "When your father died, was your brother's abusive behavior more frequent toward your mother."

Meg looked very uncomfortable. "I had to make sure when he was home, I was there too. Mom was very scared at the end. I put her in assistant living where she could be protected from him."

Ann was confused with her comment. *Who's end? Rick's end? Meg had said he was sixteen when he drowned. Had their mother been in assisted living since then?* Before Ann could continue to get some clarity, Meg appeared to become very flustered.

Meg quickly changed the subject. "You know, Dr Weise, I can see how our childhoods were so screwed up." She laughed nervously. "It makes me sad that Rick died, but it has to be a relief to my mom too." Meg looked at her watch and started to gather up her purse and keys.

Meg was obviously eager to leave, and Ann didn't want her to feel cornered. Whatever Meg was hiding would have to remain hidden for now. "Well, our time is up for today, see you next week then." Ann smiled and stood up to open the door for her to leave.

Ann's office window overlooked their parking lot with a beautiful view of the Catalina Mountains. Ann stood looking over the vista. Meg appeared from under the entrance awning and walked across to a little red Cooper parked under one of the two shade trees in the lot. She was on her cell phone and looked very agitated as she leaned against the car finishing her conversation. A few minutes later she got into the car and drove away. In all the time Meg had been seeing her, she never mentioned being in a relationship. Ann wondered who she was talking so intently to on the phone. Did she have anyone to share her fears with other than Randy?

To keep from forgetting details from their session, Ann was meticulous with her notes. She included the body language she had observed. There were moments when Meg displayed nervous movements or with a slip of the tongue, caught herself. Something was definitely going on in Meg's life. Something that was triggering her new behavior. Meg missed her session the following week.

# Karen

Karen didn't have time to miss the boys, but if it hadn't been for them, she would never have thought about returning home. She loved San Francisco. Mathew met her with open arms at the airport. They hugged each other and jumped up and down like kids. They did not come from a demonstrative family, but Mathew and Karen's affection for each other hadn't changed. They had received little affection, except for Meme. She would give the best hugs and her genuine love would light up her face just as Mathew's did as he welcomed her.

She had forgotten about slow commuting time in the Bay Area. What should have been a short drive to his apartment took over an hour. As they sat in the car among the bumper-to-bumper traffic they chatted away. Karen brought him up to speed about the boys and all their activities. As Mathew listened, he seemed to take the traffic delay in stride. He was so different from Jack. Jack would be cursing and laying heavily on the horn five minutes into the drive. Mathew did not ask about Jack or their parents and Karen didn't bring them up as well.

When they finally did arrive at the apartment, Mathew took his sister's suitcase and she followed him into the four-plex building. Mathew explained that they were paying a fortune for the small apartment, but it was worth it because it had a one-car garage. Parking in the city was a nightmare. The guys used public transportation to and from work. They kept the one car for out-of-town use and Mathew said, "Special VIPs like you that come into town via the airport."

The apartment footprint was a small one bedroom with a pull-out couch in the living room for guests. It had a tiny kitchen and a cute patio area with a barbeque. There wasn't much more than that. The minute Karen stepped inside, she felt right at home. It was like being enveloped in a cozy little haven. It was very casual and tastefully decorated.

Wonderful photos of Mathew and Greg's smiling faces greeted you from a shelf interspersed with books. Karen removed one from the shelf and asked, "Where was this taken?"

Looking over her shoulder, Mathew spoke, "Oh, that was when we were in Amsterdam last year. We make sure we get away from the craziness of life at least once a year to just be together. We both look forward to taking turns surprising each other with a location. We tell each other what type of clothes to pack but not where we are going until we get to the terminal."

Karen was enamored with the idea. "What fun! How long have you been doing this?"

Mathew smiled broadly. "About five years now. The year before that I took us to the Greek islands for a week. It was amazing, really."

"Mathew, that is just so romantic, I love it!"

A voice from the entry was heard. "What is so romantic and is it me that is so amazing?"

Karen turned to face Greg's beaming smile. She threw her arms around him. "You, you, romantic man." She pushed him back to scan his body and announce, "You look wonderful. Almost as yummy as Mathew. San Francisco certainly agrees with you both."

Greg laughed and declared, "You look pretty hot yourself."

Mathew kissed Greg hello. "I hope both of you are starving. I made reservations at one of our favorite restaurants for dinner."

The evening got even better as they laughed and spoke of memories shared together in college. Mathew talked about the thoughts that went through his mind when Karen had orchestrated his blind date with Greg. Then Greg made them laugh retelling his first impression of Mathew. "I thought he was a nerd. He kept pushing up his glasses on the bridge of his nose the whole night. I was surprised he didn't have a pocket shield with pen attached."

Mathew gave Greg a playful frown. "Oh really?" He turned to his sister. "Mister wonderful didn't tell you that he forgot his wallet in the car that night? Yours truly paid for dinner."

Greg chuckled and beamed at his partner. "Two dates later that was all forgotten in the throes of wild passion."

Karen loved the ease of banter between them and the love for each was strong and very apparent. She was so happy for them and loved feeling a connection to their lives.

They talked about mutual college friends that Karen no longer kept in touch with and friends that they hadn't thought of in years. It was a wonderful evening.

Later while lying in the pull-out-couch-bed, Karen looked back at her first day's visit. She had a mix of emotions. She was so enjoying being here with the guys. They were easy and comfortable and had no need to impress. They were obviously crazy about each other and it showed in their content life together. Of course, the comparison to her life couldn't be more opposite. Suddenly, she was overwhelmed with sadness. There was nothing meaningful in her life. Her marriage was a joke. She never felt she could be herself with Jack or her parents. Their need to impress replaced any happiness in their lives. That suffocating environment was what she was living daily.

During the next two days of carefree sightseeing and freedom, she had an opportunity to be alone with Mathew. They were walking on the beach when Mathew asked what was obvious to him. "Karen, what's going on? There are moments during the day I think you might just start crying." The air was frigid and the wind biting. Karen protectively drew her coat tightly around herself. Mathew hugged and pulled her to him for warmth. "Let's go get some coffee." He smiled down at her.

They sat in a café warming their hands around hot coffee mugs. Karen was not sure how much she was comfortable with sharing. She didn't want to burden him with her sadness, but with her first sentence tears streamed down her face, and with the flood of her tears came the flood of her grief. "Mathew I am—" She wiped away the tears with a napkin. "I am so miserable. My life is in shambles. My marriage isn't a marriage. Jack has been cheating on me for a long time now. Mom and Dad, well hell, you know what they are like—" She pointed to the beach across the street. "They are as cold as the fog outside."

Mathew covered her hand with his, sadly he looked at his sister and said, "Don't stop. Tell me everything."

She took a deep breath and continued. "I'm so trapped! Damn it! I'm barely hanging on. I decided to leave Jack and I know there will be no support from Mom and Dad." She stopped and really heard her words ring true for Mathew as well. "You of all people understand. You came out to them and they were finished with you."

Mathew nodded and the pain on his face was for her pain too. He squeezed her hand. "Karen, I will always be here for you. So, let's start sorting this all out."

Karen gathered her thoughts and explained her plan to get a job and secure herself for getting custody of the boys. She told him her plan to open an account of her own and start shoving as much money as she can into it.

Mathew held up his hand to interrupt her and smiled. "Remember, please, your brother is a financial advisor. We will get you into a high return fund right away." Before she could speak, he continued, "And, before you even start to object, I am going to put some money into it and get all this rolling." He could see her ready to say no. He cut her off before she could speak. "Okay, so that is the first step, now before we continue, I just want to say this weekend has made me realize just how much I've missed you. We need each other, Karen. You, the boys, Greg and me. We will be our own little family here in the Bay Area. The hell with them, they have never been our family."

It was music to Karen's ears. Finally, there was a ray of light. "Mathew, I cannot tell you what a heavy weight you have taken off of me, just to be able to have you to talk to and confide in. I think before we make this plan, shouldn't you check with Greg first. Perhaps he would rather not be that close to me and the boys?"

"That won't be a problem, I can assure you." Mathew's face lit up and with an ear to ear smile he announced, "Greg and I would love to have Aunt Karen and cousins close by for the child we are in the process of adopting."

Karen was so happy for them. Tears of joy welled up in her eyes. "Oh, Oh! Mathew, that is amazing. You will be the best parents ever!"

Mathew was the most focused person she knew and after sharing the happy news about the adoption, he went right back to making sure that she understood how he was here to support her. "What is going on in your head right now? There is something else going on in your life, isn't there?"

"At times I am so confident that I can do this and then there are times—" Karen struggled with how to tell him. "Mathew, my confidence is at the lowest point in my life. Something happened to me and since then, sometimes I'm scared to even leave the house." In a low, fragile voice, she said. "I was beaten and raped."

Mathew felt a rush of shock, anger, and outrage overtake him. He stared into Karen's eyes and in a fierce voice said, "If it was Jack, so help me God, I will kill him!"

"No, no, it wasn't Jack, he doesn't even know. No one does, except now you." She proceeded to tell him everything about that horrible night. They talked for hours, and Karen finally opened the floodgate of emotions that she had been unable to share with anyone else.

# Ann

Tomorrow Meg was scheduled to come in for her appointment. Ann was concerned that she would skip it again as she had last week. Something had definitely shifted in Meg's mind, which, if not explored, could jeopardize all the work they had done over the last year. She once again studied her notes on Meg from their last meeting. She was trying to zero in on something she may have missed.

She glanced at the clock, noting her next appointment time was in a few minutes. A new patient was being seen and a folder had been prepared and placed on her desk. Ann reviewed it briefly. She was thirty-eight, married with two children. Other than a name, there was very little more than an address and billing information, which was typical.

Peggy checked to see if Ann was ready for the appointment and then opened her door to announce. "Mrs Michael, this is Dr Weise." Karen walked in and Peggy closed the door behind her and returned to the reception desk.

The last time they had met, they both looked very different, having been beaten and raped. Karen took a seat on the couch, not yet making the connection. Ann knew who she was right away. Ann wasn't sure what she was feeling. Her chest tightened, and their attacker's face flashed in her mind. Remembering again; how hard this woman had fought to get away from him. It was if slides of those images were flashing in her head, Ann's second reaction was to reach out and hug her, but instead she said. "This is very awkward. We have met before."

Karen studied Ann's face for the briefest of moments before she realized who Ann was. Her trembling hand covered her mouth and in a quiet, shaky voice, she said "Oh, my." Karen too was in shock. She continued to stare at her while images of Addie stabbing that man to death made her slightly dizzy and nauseous. The silence between them lingered a few seconds longer.

Ann was not at all sure how to proceed. "I have never been in a professional situation like this before. I'm not sure if we should—" Ann stopped to clear her mind from the shock of seeing Karen there in front of her. "Karen, I believe I know why you are here." A nervous and uncomfortable chuckle followed.

Karen smiled and said, "Yes, I believe you do."

Ann instantly liked her. "I feel, professionally, I can't continue having this a session, but I very much want to know if this is the first time you have sought help with this."

"Yes, it is. My brother insisted I start dealing with it."

Ann vigorously nodded her head. "I'm so glad that you are. Under the circumstances, I would like to suggest that you see my colleague here in the office. She is excellent and I'm sure you will feel very comfortable talking with her. Although I will not be your therapist, I need you to know that this meeting is in confidence and will not be shared with anyone, including my colleague if you choose to see her."

Karen began to relax. "Thank you, I will make an appointment with her on my way out." She continued with, "Dr Weise, I have to ask, how are you doing?"

Ann was very touched by her concern. "First of all, it's Ann and thank you for asking. I am very lucky to have a wonderful support system. You mentioned your brother. Obviously, I don't know him, but I'm so happy he is a support for you."

Karen stood up to leave and Ann came from behind her desk. Their handshake turned into a hug that lingered. It was an intensely meaningful, reassuring, and connecting moment for both of them.

Karen left the office and Ann sat down on her couch and stared at her desk in front of her. From this perspective, suddenly she had a great appreciation and respect for the strength it took for her patients to reach out for help. She felt a twinge of shame not having done so herself. It had been almost a year since the rape, and it was a comfort to Ann to know Karen was finally seeking help. It was too late for Addie. *It might be time for me as well.*

Later that evening, dinner was planned for Nicky and Ann to finally meet Brad. Kate had been seeing him almost a month now. Nicky was running late at the hospital and would be meeting them at the restaurant. It had been a very emotional day for Ann. Meeting Karen had been so unexpected she was looking forward to sharing the experience with Nicky.

Ann went home to shower and dress for dinner. She arrived at the restaurant, Brad and Kate had already found them a table. Kate made the introductions. Ann could see why Kate was attracted to him. He was definitely Kate's type. He had that carefree look and was casually dressed. Brad's ginger hair complimented his blue-green eyes. They sparkled when he smiled, which he did as he shook Ann's hand. He had a medium build, but his short-sleeve shirt fitted snugly around his biceps. Ann smiled to herself, and *yes, he did smell good.*

Nicky had taken the bus so she could drive home with Ann. She arrived shortly after Ann and the introductions took place once again. Nicky leaned over Ann, kissing her quickly and sat down beside her. They were all hungry and immediately picked up their menus and made their choices. Once the orders were placed conversation began. Nicky addressed Brad. "Kate mentioned you work at Tucson Medical Center. What do you do?"

"Oh, right, she told me you're a surgeon there. I'm in the ER, triage. I'm surprised we never ran into each other. How long have you been there?"

Nicky took a sip of her water. "It's been—" She tilted her head and looked toward Ann. "It's been five years." Ann nodded. Nicky asked him the same question.

"I got here two years ago. I like it there. I like Tucson in general. It has a small town feel even through it's so spread out. You can't beat the scenery. People are really friendly here. I'm still getting used to the heat, but I'm in an air-conditioned hospital most of the time. I'm catching on, that summers, are going from air-conditioned house to air-conditioned car to air-conditioned work."

Ann chuckled. "Well, you are a true Tucsonan now, but the rest of the year is amazing weather. Where are you from originally?"

Brad talked about the small town he grew up north of Chicago. He talked about his close-knit family and attending Northwestern University. The rest of the evening was enjoyed with easy interaction and getting to know Brad.

On the way home Nicky and Ann agreed that they liked him and could see that he made Kate happy. As Nicky drove them home, Ann texted that they had approved of him and could picture Kate smiling at her phone.

They had barely gotten in the house and Ann immediately told her about Karen walking into her office earlier in the day. Nicky's face registered shock. "Wow! That had to have been really weird for both of you."

"Oh my God, it was. At first it was awkward to say the least, but, honey, it was also kind of—" Ann searched for the right word. "Healing, no, that isn't it. It was comforting." Ann's forehead wrinkled in concentration. "She was there in front of me, there was an instant connection between us. There was an intimacy almost, we had shared something that would always connect us. Does that make sense to you? It's kind of confusing for me to sort out how I really feel."

Nicky looked deeply into her eyes. "It perfectly makes sense to me. Did you tell Kate?"

"I can't discuss her at all with Kate, which will be very frustrating. It looks like Karen will be seeing her. I know Kate will be able to help her and that is much more important."

# CHAPTER 5
## Karen

Jack was talking but her head was spinning with what had taken place at Ann's office. She still found it hard to believe. *What was the chance of that?* She couldn't wait to tell Mathew.

Jack looked annoyed. "Earth to Karen. You need to be at the office in the morning." Karen redirected her focus. "Sorry. What did you say?"

He rolled his eyes. "The au pair candidate, you need to come to the office in the morning for the video interview. You said you wanted to be a part of the process."

*Why was he making this so formal?* "Jack, can't we do this from home instead of your office? I have a second interview for a job in the morning."

Annoyed he said, "Karen, I have a busy day tomorrow and I might have to stay late at the office. I don't have time to constantly rearrange my schedule."

"Well, that's my point. I can rearrange the interview from here and it doesn't have to be tomorrow. Or I can just interview her myself." The minute the second part of her statement was out of her mouth, she knew she had made a big no-no. Taking away his power and, God forbid, the woman was older and unattractive.

In a voice that read instant rejection, "No." He hesitated and then half conceded with, "Very well, we will do this on Friday at my office. Make sure your day is cleared."

*Clear my day!* Before starting another confrontation, she controlled her building anger. "Jack, if I'm to get this job, you are going to have to check with me before setting appointments involving me." She was sure he wasn't happy that the playing field was changing in the house. *Too damn bad, he'd better get used to it.*

Not wanting to look as if she had made her point, he waved his hand dismissively and with a scowl said, "Fine. I'll let you know the time on Friday." Making sure his was the last word, he added as he left the room, "Make sure you are available when it's set."

*Screw you, master! You never even asked about what the job interview was for.* Karen couldn't tell if it was more of Jack's self-absorption or he wanted to hurt her and belittle her importance. She concluded it was all of that.

The first job interview had not been as intimidating as she had feared. This second one was, nonetheless, making her nervous. The position was for an office manager/assistant with a non-profit children's organization. Her organizational skills got her through the first interview with the present office manager,

Rosa, who was doing the initial interviewing for her own replacement starting in two weeks. She had been a pleasant and efficient woman who gave Karen a very good idea of what her responsibilities would entail. Seeing what Rosa did gave Karen an opportunity to think through possible questions she may be asked in the second interview with the director.

Rosa had been casual and inviting like her office. Based on that, Karen laid out what she felt would be appropriate clothes to fit into that setting for tomorrow's second interview. After she and Jack had their brief but infuriating discussion, he retreated to his office-bedroom and she to the master bedroom to call Mathew on her cell.

She could almost picture Mathew's face of amazement at hearing about Ann Weise. In retelling him the details of their encounter she was able to reexamine the thoughts that had gone through her head at the time. At the very moment that she realized who Ann was, she had felt the need to stand up and escape. Her shock was the only thing that paralyzed her from doing so. In telling him her gut reaction, in retrospect, she was able to clarify what she was actually feeling. It wasn't Ann. It was the whole experience of that night that surged through her with blinding fear. She continued to explain to him that after her pounding heart began to slow down, she had a sense of calm. This woman in front of her totally knew her. At that moment, Ann knew more about her than anyone else in her life, except for Mathew. Thinking back to that instant realization was such a convoluted thought. After all, she and Ann were perfect strangers, really. The meeting was an overload of emotions and feelings she did not yet understand completely.

It was so comforting being able to release all these feeling with Mathew. He was such good support and a caring listener. Unlike her husband, Mathew was excited for her with the news that she had gotten a second interview. He reassured her that he was sure that was a good sign. He told her just to be herself. With his encouragement, Karen was starting to regain a sense of who that was.

The director stood up from his office chair and came around his desk to greet Karen. He met her with a warm, open smile and motioned her to have a seat in one of the worn easy chairs that made her think of Meme's house. Neither Karen's nor the chair he sat in matched. His desk was one of those metal monstrosities from the nineteen-fifties. There was nothing fancy about his makeshift office. She liked that the furnishings were secondhand. It spoke to her that perhaps the money was being spent for the children and not going into the pockets of the administrators. She liked also that he addressed her by her first name.

"Welcome, Karen. I'm Doug." He got right to the point. "Rosa has been with me from the beginnings of this organization. She and I work well together, I will miss her. I trust her completely in determining who she feels is qualified to replace her." He laughed. "So, actually, if Rosa feels you have the skills, then I'm good with that. My part here is to get to know you and see how we both feel about working together."

Then they just talked. They talked about themselves, and she was free to ask him questions as well. He was a short man whom she guessed to be in his late sixties. His hair was mostly gray, but Karen judged his age by his hands. They were weathered and told a story of a man who had worked hard during his life. Based on their easy and sometimes humorous conversation, her observations had been right. He grew up on a ranch that his family still owned in the outskirts of Tucson. It was there he was taught the meaning of a work ethic. When he retired, he wasn't one to be sedentary, so he started volunteering at the local school to work with children. It was then that he learned the needed resources and opportunities were often lacking in these children's lives and he started this organization.

Karen really liked Doug and their ease of conversation stretched beyond his allotted time with her. They were mutually comfortable with each other. So, she was hired, and Karen would begin training with Rosa in a week.

It became apparent that Jack had already interviewed prior candidates for the au pair position. He had narrowed down his choices. Karen was now in Jack's office for the interview. It became instantly transparent that this was not the first time he was speaking with *his* choice. The woman before them on the screen was very attractive. *What a surprise*, was Karen's first thought.

Her name was Jamie and she was from Canada. Jamie was fresh out of college and this would be her first job. At least, thought Karen, Jack had found her through a reputable agency. She seemed to be articulate and pleasant. Karen asked her questions about her experience with children and was satisfied with her responses. Jamie was amicable with including French lessons with the boys as part of their homework routine. Karen discussed with her the boys' schedules and clearly covered what responsibilities would be required from her, as well as what she was not expected to do. Jack obviously hadn't a clue on that subject nor had laid out the hours for Jamie's own private weekend and evening time. Jamie seemed pleased that Karen was clear and addressed other details that had not been previously discussed with Jack. She assured Karen she understood that situations would come up with two working parents and she had no problem being flexible. Karen asked her if she was comfortable with what they had discussed and if Jamie had any concerns or questions. Jamie brought up the fact that she did not own and would require a vehicle. Jack jumped in and said he would see to that right away.

Karen was not interested in the discussions Jack previously had had with the agency nor details of

Jamie's salary or room and board. She was confident the agency represented their client fairly.

It was news to Jack when Karen announced to Jamie that she would be starting to train for her new job in one week. Karen asked her if that was workable. Jamie was available right away, and could be there next weekend in time for Jamie to settle in before Karen started work.

With the conference call over, Jack said he needed to get ready for his next appointment and Karen was *excused.* He had yet to ask about her new job.

## Ann

Her caseload was heavy, but Ann was glad to see Meg's session had not been cancelled today. When Meg arrived, she looked pale and washed out. She had never before come to Ann's office without makeup and today it had not been applied. Her usually brushed and lovely hair hung limply around her face.

Meg didn't sit on the couch, her usual choice; instead, she dropped into an easy chair. Ann sat in her armchair facing her. Meg looked at Ann through reddened, tired eyes. Ann did not mask her concern. "Meg, you are not looking well. Are you ill?" Meg looked too tired to cry but Ann could sense it might happen any moment.

Without preface she stated, "Dr Weise, I lied to you. Now I need your help more than ever."

Ann had already suspected from their last session that Meg had not been forthcoming about her situation. Meg was, however, no longer nervous or agitated, she simply looked exhausted. Ann knew from Meg's directness she did not have to ease her into conversation. She didn't have to wait longer than a slight hesitation before Meg continued. "I told you that my brother died at sixteen," she stated very bluntly. "He did not. He died just over a year ago. Or at least I thought he had." She leaned back into the couch, settling in for the unveiling of her lies.

Ann could hear the hoarseness in Meg's weary voice. From the metal pitcher of ice water on her desk, Ann poured a glass and handed it to her. Meg took a sip of the water and placed the glass on the end table beside her. She began again. "You see, all my life, I would picture ways in which Rick could die. They were like little scenarios playing out in my mind." The slightest hint of a confessional smile crossed her face. "As you already know, my favorite being by drowning. It was the less violent and the least problematic, I guess you might say." Meg stopped talking and seemed to be off in some memory.

Ann didn't want to stop the momentum that had begun so she said, "You mentioned that you thought be had died about a year ago, but he hadn't. Can you tell me about that?"

Meg looked up at Ann, her face was tired looking. "Rick had been in some kind of bad fight and was seriously injured. He was rushed to the hospital." Meg's face changed from weariness to anger. "You see, Dr Weise? I thought he was dead." She was now angered. "Why! It could have all been over, finally over." She shook her head sadly. "The doctors said he was dead, his heart had stopped, but they pulled him back from death. God, if Randy and I had just walked away, but we didn't. It could have ended the nightmare we lived with all our lives. I could finally have a normal life, maybe even a boyfriend."

"Did you feel Randy betrayed you?"

Meg nodded vigorously. "I did! I always said someday we would stop saving Rick. We promised each other next time he was in trouble we—" She did not finish her sentence but it's meaning was clear.

"It has been months of rehab and throughout it all I wished he would get some complication and die. I'm angry at myself too. I could have done something to end it when it was at its worst in the hospital, overdose him, or something, anything, but I wasn't brave enough."

Ann found the opportunity to point out, "Perhaps you can understand that Randy too was not brave enough."

Meg begrudgingly admitted she did understand. "The thing is, Rick got out of the hospital meaner than ever. He moved in with Mom." Pain registered across her face. "That wasn't good, Mom was getting hurt. So, I put her in an assisted living place. He started coming there. Finally, they told him he couldn't come back there to visit her. He would yell at her and even other patients, and they were afraid he might hit Mom or someone else. I'm still afraid he will try to retaliate by doing something to the place." Meg released a rush of bottled-up stress with a rush of air from her lungs. "Randy thinks he's in some kind of trouble again, but Rick won't say what he's doing. It was so calm and peaceful while he was in the hospital sedated for those months."

Ann now had the puzzle pieces of the past year's sessions with Meg. "Although you are incapable of killing your brother, your guilt remains the same for wanting him dead." Ann leaned forward in her chair. "Meg, you and Randy are suffering from guilt about *feelings,* not actions. We all have bad thoughts and feelings, feeling about things we would never do in real life. You are still battling with guilt because that is all you've known. Your whole life, you and Randy could only try to repair damage Rick caused, not prevent it. Nothing has changed. You understandably are reverting back to *death as the solution* and feeling guilty for those thoughts." Ann stopped talking to let Meg consider her words.

Tears pooled and then streaked down her cheek. "It would be the solution, if he had died, I mean. I just can't take much more." She put her face in her hands and sobbed. Ann put the tissue box in Meg's lap and took her seat once more. Meg wiped her eyes and blew her runny nose. "We don't know what to do about Rick. One of these days he is going to kill someone."

Ann ached for Meg's feeling of fear. "I know that you logically understand that there is nothing you can do to prevent something from happening in the future. But basically, you and Randy coped as children by projecting into the future the opportunity for his death, which would be your freedom. Once at the hospital, you could not go through with the fantasy of finishing him off. Your fantasies have not been able to save you. Now you realize having had the opportunity, you are incapable of playing them out. You never were capable."

Meg looked up at Ann through blurry tear-filled eyes. Meg's eyes were begging Ann for a solution. "I know you are saying when we were kids, we shouldn't have been made to feel responsible for what Rick got into. But what about now? What do I do?"

"You have already done it. You have made sure your mother is safe from him. If you need to, you will place her in another facility. You are in the present and can only deal with protecting her. You cannot protect him now any more than you could as a child."

Meg's face was heavy with sadness. "I'm exhausted."

Ann nodded in agreement. "Yes. You have been most of your life. You and your brother are responsible for protecting yourselves and your mother. You *are not* responsible for protecting the world from Rick. That is not your guilt to own."

Meg took a deep breath and slowly released it. "It's like always waiting for a time bomb to go off."

Ann thought that was a perfect analogy for Meg's life. "We are out of time today, but next week let's talk about that feeling." Ann stood at the window looking down to the parking lot. Once gain she watched Meg get into her little red car and drive away. She felt so badly for Meg but at the same time she was hopeful that Meg was finally ready to make real progress.

# Karen

It had been a month now and Karen was really happy with her job. The training had gone well. Rosa was an excellent instructor. She was organized and efficient and left the office in shape so that Karen was ready to start right after training. She and Doug worked well together and at the beginning of the third week, he gave her another responsibility, which only built her confidence.

Things had fallen in place at home as well. Jamie had arrived as planned. It gave Karen time to get to know her and to settle Jamie in with her duties before starting her own job. Most importantly, the boys liked her. Jack was rarely home again, which made everyone's life easier. Jamie had the privacy she needed in the second master suite, which had been their guest suite. Karen had asked Jamie to lunch and they went shopping to get a few things to make her space cozier. Jamie was very touched that Karen had taken that extra effort to make her comfortable.

Karen's highlight of each week was the telephone call with Mathew. She was so much happier, and she couldn't wait to report how her week had gone and ask him about his. She was very excited to hear that the adoption process, although slower than hoped, was moving along. The little girl was from China and she was nine months old. Mathew was concerned that they would be missing so many of the *firsts*. He and Greg wanted her with them for her first steps, her first everything. Karen wanted her savings to grow faster so she and the boys could be there as soon as possible and bond with her as soon as the guys could get her.

Karen had started dinner when Jack walked into the kitchen. Of course, Karen never knew when or if he would be home. There was never a hello or how was your day.

Jamie and JJ were quietly working in the adjacent room that Karen could see from her vantage point in the kitchen. Jack put his briefcase down on the counter and took off his suit jacket. "Tell Jamie to pick up my good suit at the cleaners tomorrow." Jamie and JJ were out of Jack's line of sight. Jamie looked up meeting Karen's eyes.

Karen continued chopping up the red pepper and calmly stated, "Jack, that isn't one of Jamie's responsibilities."

He tilted his head and sarcastically asked, "Well, what the hell did I hire her for then?"

Karen put the knife down and gave him her full attention. She wanted Jamie to hear this as well. "Jamie is not our maid, Jack. You were in the same interview I was when her responsibilities were discussed. She is responsible for getting the boys to and from school and all their outside sports and activities. If the boys are sick or need to see a doctor and we are not available, she knows where the pediatrician office is located." *I'm sure you haven't a clue where the doctor was or even her name,* she thought. "I will pick up your suit on my way home from work tomorrow."

"I bought a damn car for her! I don't think it's such a fucking deal." Karen saw from the corner of her eye that JJ's head had turned toward their conversation taking place in the kitchen. His face had turned red in embarrassment of his father's comment.

"The car is needed for Jamie to do *her* job."

Karen had put Jack in his place calmly and politely. It didn't matter, he wasn't happy. He could never let anything go without needing the last word. When that happened, he usually just got nastier. He waved a threatening finger in Karen face. "You better remember I still run this house. Since you started that job of yours you think your shit don't stink. You better get off your high horse. You and that sweet little piece of ass upstairs do not run me." JJ looked directly at his mother. His face was red with embarrassment. Jamie looked down at the opened book they had been studying together.

Mark must have heard his father's voice from upstairs and ran down. "Hey, Dad, cool, you're home. Want to play catch?"

As if a switch had been turned off, Jack smiled broadly at his son. "You bet, little buddy; I'll go change." Obviously thinking JJ was in his room he said, "Go upstairs and tell your brother. I'll meet you guys in the backyard." Jack headed to his study.

Karen glanced at Jamie and JJ at the dining room table. They both were avoiding eye contact. They collected their work and JJ took it and went upstairs. Jamie came into the kitchen and washed her hands in the sink next to Karen. Turning to Karen, she said, "I think I might catch a movie and dinner in town this evening."

Karen nodded and said to her as she was leaving the kitchen, "I need you to know that I greatly appreciate how well you do your job. If Jack asks of you *anything* you feel uncomfortable doing, come to me immediately." Karen's message had been received perfectly clear by Jamie.

Karen wondered what was going on in JJ's mind and heart right now. She ached for him. He was mature for his age and understood everything his father had said. Mark joined Jack downstairs and announced that

JJ wasn't feeling well and was staying upstairs for a while before dinner.

Karen watched Mark and Jack head for the backyard. She wiped her hands on the tea towel and went up to JJ's room. She knocked quietly and entered his room. He was laying on the bed with his arms behind his head staring at the ceiling. Karen sat down next to him and looked up at the constellation of reflective stars they had put up together. "They seem to be holding up there pretty good."

JJ smirked. "A few have fallen down."

Karen chuckled and stretched out beside him on the bed. "Want to talk about it?"

JJ didn't respond right away, but finally in anger he said, "You know what really makes me mad?" Karen just shook her head. So, he continued, "Dad always talks about working as a team with baseball, he said it's like life." His mouth curled up in one corner as he worked through his next thought. "Dad is never a team player." Karen wasn't sure what he meant but she could hear the hurt in his voice. "He says sports are important because it teaches you good stuff like how to treat others fair."

*Fairly, but this not the time to correct his grammar.* "JJ, I'm not going to defend your father because I agree with you. I just want to make sure that you understood that sometimes people say and do things that are wrong. It's important to recognize those times and make sure they do not become something to copy even if an adult does it."

"There are a lot of things Dad does that make me mad. He embarrasses me too sometimes. That was really bad what he said about Jamie. She's really nice."

"She is. She is very nice. Sometimes words can really hurt. They can hurt just like someone was hitting you. You know we taught you that you are never to hit a girl. I think that is how Jamie felt tonight."

"Sometimes he hits you that way too. It makes me so angry."

Karen was unaware that he and perhaps Mark had seen Jack and her at their worst. "Honey, I'm sorry I didn't know you and your brother have heard us fighting. Sometimes, parents fight. All families have–"

Impatiently he said, "I know that, Mom! But Dad doesn't fight fair. He says stuff that is mean to you and puts you down. He's a bully, and he thinks I don't know that. He's not a bully to me and Mark, but he is to you. He doesn't treat boys bad, but he does girls."

Karen felt ashamed. Jack was not the example she wants for her boys, and she is just as guilty for allowing the boys to see her as an example of putting up with Jack's behavior. "You mean to me and now Jamie?"

JJ looked at her sheepishly. In a quieter voice he continued, "One time when Dad came to my game… I saw him behind the bleachers. He pushed this lady up against the back of the snack shop wall and she had to slap him to get him away from her. Then he called her the B word."

Her whole chest ached for her son. "Oh, JJ, I am so sorry you had to see something like that." She sat up and caressed his soft baby face with her hand. "I promise you I will not let your father treat me or Jamie like that. I promise you I will have much more respect for myself. Almost as much respect as I have for you right now. I don't always notice how grown up you are. I can hardly believe you are twelve already. I want you to know how proud I am of you and the young man you are becoming."

He said he didn't want to come down for dinner, so Karen brought his dinner to his room. Jack was the father of the year to Mark during dinner. Karen could see the worship in Mark's eyes when he looked at Jack. It worried her. She planned to discuss it with Kate at her therapy session this week.

Jack went right back into his home office as soon as dinner was over. Karen finished cleaning up the kitchen. She opened the office door without knocking. She stood in the doorway and before he even looked up, she said, "You are never to speak to me that way again, Jack. I'm sorry you are pissed that I will not sleep with you. Frankly, in that area you disgust me. I can't sleep with the man I no longer respect or can be respected by. That is beside the point. The point is, as the mother of your children, you *will* respect me. Your affairs are of no concern to me any longer. But I'm telling you right now, if you make a move on Jamie, I will personally help her bring charges against you. You are not to even communicate with her. Her duties will be totally handled by me. The boys like her and you are not going to screw this up for them. You and your sexual needs are to be conducted outside of this house and family."

She didn't wait for a response. She closed his door and went to her bedroom to call Mathew. The closest she had come to letting her tears flow was during the conversation she'd had with JJ in his room earlier. She wasn't about to let Jack see her cry when she confronted him in his office. But now she sobbed. She wasn't sure if it was from outrage or pure sadness for JJ. She finally stopped and pulled herself together. She picked up her cell phone and before she dialed, the night of the attack flashed before her.

The sudden recall of that night wasn't about the details of the violence. Those physical blows she had felt that horrible night, were no different than the slugs to her stomach she had felt tonight. She began to understand her anger and the feeling of not having control, not being able to protect herself, being a victim, all those feelings she had felt tonight. Jack was no different than that predator, and I have allowed him to be so with me. With resolve she wiped away her tears, *No, I can never feel like this again.*

# CHAPTER 6
## Ann

Ann's last patient for the day was leaving. Ann walked him out to the reception desk where she left him to schedule his next appointment. As she was returning to her office to organize her notes on their session, Karen walked in for her appointment with Kate. Ann and Karen nodded to each other and smiled. Ann had the overwhelming feeling of wanting to ask Karen to meet her for lunch. She wondered if Karen would like to get to know her as well. Talking about what had happened might be beneficial for both of them. Ann reassessed her thinking. No. Karen was doing the right thing seeking help from Kate. Wanting to reach out to Karen was self-serving and selfish. It could possibly interfere with Karen's therapy.

Ann had begun experiencing disturbing thoughts about that night at the garage again. It was more worrisome when they would take place while she was working with a patient. It was getting harder to dismiss the thoughts before they would take root and disrupt her day. It was time to make an appointment with Kate's recommended therapist. Karen had become an inspiration to her. It was time to stop pretending Nicky and Kate were all she needed. As much as she felt supported, she was alone in experiencing how it had changed her, allowing it to interfere with her life and career. It was time to stop shoving her feelings down deeper. Karen's feelings were her own to explore. *It was time to get help to figure out my own.*

After finishing up at the office, Ann went home to prepare dinner. Kate and Brad were joining them. She and Nicky really enjoyed getting to know Brad and loved seeing Kate so happy. He was funny and smart and the four of them had an easy, comfortable friendship.

Dinner never had to be fancy when Brad and Kate were over. Ann threw together a salad and made a simple garlic shrimp pasta. Kate brought dessert. They arrived as Nicky got out of the shower. With wet hair, shorts, and a T-shirt she sat down and dinner was placed on the table family style. Ann smiled as she watched Nicky pile the pasta on her plate. She was always amazed at her partner's voracious appetite that never showed on her petite frame. Kate smiled and said, "Ever since I've known you, you can devour a meal in minutes no matter how much is on your plate."

Nicky shrugged her shoulders. "I think med school did that to me. You had to catch a meal on the run and there was never enough time to eat."

"Right?" Brad enthusiastically agreed. "I remember having to do that too." He laughed. "But I just got major indigestion. You must have multiple stomachs like a cow." Nicky slugged him in the arm, and they all laughed. "I'm just saying I am in awe of you, girl."

Nicky leaned back in her chair and pushed her empty plate aside as the others continued their meal. "Speaking of the hospital. Man, you guys must have been swamped in the ER today. We had emergency surgeries all day long."

Brad nodded and finished what he was chewing. "We really did. There was a pile up on Interstate Ten. We saw some nasty shit today. A few were DOA." He wiped his mouth with his napkin. "In the middle of all the craziness, this guy comes in with a real bad attitude and wants to be stitched up right away. He had a deep cut that needed stitching, but he was far down the list of triages today. I remembered this guy. About a year ago he was brought in in really bad shape. Multiple stab wounds. They took him right to you guys." Brad pointed to Nicky with his fork. "I was surprised when he walked in that he had survived."

Ann's stomach felt nauseous. The stabbing that took place in the garage flashed into her mind. Ann first felt angry and hurt that they could talk so nonchalantly about this in front of her, although this kind of shop talk wasn't anything new for the four of them when they got together. She tried to bury her feelings and thoughts like she had been since they had started tormenting her again. They were beginning to paralyze her from moving on. *This has to stop. I can't keep having these flashbacks. I need to really make an appointment with the therapist in the morning.*

Nicky and Brad went into the living room to continue their conversation while Ann and Kate were cleaning up in the kitchen. Kate looked at Ann standing beside her at the sink. With a concerned voice she asked, "What's going on with you?"

Ann and Kate were much too close not to pick up on each other's mood and body language. Ann smiled tightly. "I'm failing at dealing with the rape. The scar isn't healing very well. It's not happening for me." She turned and faced Kate. "Tonight—"

Kate finished her sentence for her. "Tonight, you had a bad flashback."

Ann's shoulders dropped in defeat. "They are happening more often. I can't afford to let it jeopardize our practice. I'll call in the morning for an appointment. What is his name again?"

"It's a her. Marty Stein, honey, she's good."

After the evening was over with their guests, Nicky and Ann cuddled on the couch to watch a movie. Ann let herself be immersed in the comedy. They went to bed late and Nicky was out in five minutes. Ann remained unable to sleep with her thoughts darting around her head like fish. *Why am I feeling like a failure? Asking for help is a brave thing to do. My patients do it every day.* She went with that question to herself, as a psychiatrist it didn't take long to connect this feeling to her dad. She couldn't fix him either. Morning came very suddenly after sleeping only a couple of hours. Nicky had already left for the hospital. Ann dragged herself into the shower.

Luckily, her schedule of appointments for the day was light. She finished up on some paperwork. She took the slip of paper Kate had given her months ago out of the back of her desk drawer. She stared at Dr Stein's name on the Post-it note. Kate said that Dr Stein only saw rape victims and women who suffered from abuse. She took a sip of her third cup of coffee of the day and dialed the number.

The receptionist on the other end of the call greeted Ann professionally. She did not ask Ann her name. Instead, she asked her if she was suicidal.

Ann was momentarily taken aback. "No. No I'm not. I would like to make an appointment with Dr Stein." It was then that Ann understood that Brad dealt with one type of triage, this was another. Once again, Ann wasn't prepared to hear the receptionist say that Dr Stein had a cancellation that afternoon and would Ann like to take that session? She had procrastinated for months and she knew if she didn't take the appointment, she would keep putting it off, so she took the three-thirty opening.

Dr Stein was not far from Ann's office. Her office was set up not unlike her own. She sat in the waiting area filling out paperwork of general questions and billing information.

Dr Stein met her with a handshake and smile and invited her to take a seat. Ann chose a comfortable chair. Ann's gaydar kicked in and she knew Marty Stein was gay. She was slim and athletically built, around five-six. Her asymmetrical hair was cropped short. She had a nice smile that showed straight, even teeth that either she or her parents had spent some big money on.

She spoke first. "Since I haven't yet read your paperwork, why don't you tell me about yourself."

Ann kept it general and brief. "My name is Ann Weise, I'm a psychiatrist as well. I have a practice not far from you. My partner and I have been together thirteen years. My life partner, that is."

Dr Stein waited to make sure that Ann's brief introduction was done. And then she said, "And you are here because you have been raped." It was a statement and not a question. Ann just nodded. Marty Stein continued. "Okay." Which was stated as if that had been established. "How long ago was the rape and why have you come to see me?"

Dr Stein's approach to therapy was very different from her own. She obviously just got to the point. "It's been a little over a year and I'm beginning to have frequent flashbacks. I don't want them interfering with my work… frankly my life as well."

"Ann… may I call you Ann?" Ann nodded. "Good, you can call me Marty. As you know in our profession, we spend a great deal of time easing our patients into opening up to us. It's time consuming and frankly frustrating that you can't get to the heart of their issues and start the healing process. I know everyone needs their own time and space to peel back the layers. So, choose a pace that is comfortable and let's get to work. Let me know about your past, let me know how you see yourself, how the rape has changed you. Open up and let me in and let me help you."

Ann took a sigh of relief and realized that part of her procrastination for all these months was from dreading the very process Marty had just put into short order. So, she began.

## Karen

Karen couldn't get Ann out of her mind since seeing her at Dr Jordan's office. During the day her mind would wander with thoughts and questions about her, like she had, when seeing Addie on the television. Somehow, however, meeting Ann made it much more intimate. She was real outside of the memories of that night. She wondered if Ann was married, did she have kids? Was she a good friend? Was her life fulfilling? Was she fun to be around before the rape and did that change her, and maybe she was no longer fun? The more she thought about the questions, the more she began to internalize them. *What was I like before?*

Her wandering thoughts were interrupted when her son JJ dropped his backpack on the floor. "I don't see why I have to go to some stupid lunch at the country club!"

Karen was confused. "What lunch?"

"Grandma and Dad said Mark and I have to go and have our pictures taken after."

Karen had not been involved with the club since starting to work. She rather liked it that way. Her *friends* were not all that pleased with her absence and just dropped her. She no longer felt she had anything in common with them. She didn't want to think herself a snob, but they were so shallow. There, she'd just answered one of her own questions. That was her before the rape. She saw that JJ had begun to pace. "What is the luncheon for?"

JJ looked annoyed. "He didn't tell you? Grandma said you have to be there too. He's running for councilman and he has to parade our family around for the press. It's a joke, they don't know who he really is."

*When the hell did this decision take place?* "JJ, calm down. We need to talk about your anger toward your father lately."

They heard Jack enter the foyer and JJ grabbed his backpack, rolled his eyes, and headed upstairs to his room. Karen didn't wait for Jack to come into the family room. She went to the foyer. "Jack, when were you going to tell me about you running for councilman?"

He pursed his lips and stared at her for a moment. In a snarky voice, he said, "Since you started working, we don't see each other much. We haven't connected in much anyway, even before your job." His innuendo was quite clear.

"Jack, I don't want to fight with you, but if you recall," Karen gestured quotation marks with her fingers, "*we were not seeing each other much,* was your call, not mine." She didn't wait for a response. "JJ mentioned a luncheon that we are supposed to attend." With heavy sarcasm she asked, "When is my presence needed for that?"

"It's a Sunday brunch this weekend." He started to say more but didn't press his luck and left the room.

Karen was biding her time and putting away every penny she made. She raised her budget for the family house expenses, putting a little more in her savings. She was hoping Jack would not notice. She figured she was probably safe since Jack didn't notice much that didn't concern him. Slowly but steadily, her savings were growing. Her pride would not allow her to ask Mathew if he did indeed invest some money for her. She hoped now more than ever that he had. There was even more stress since JJ had opened up to her concerning Jack. JJ's anger worried her. She recognized she had become more assertive with her interactions with Jack; she did so for herself as much as to keep her promise to JJ. But that could become a double-edged sword and turn on her. Thank God she was still was seeing Dr Kate Jordan. Other than her conversations with Mathew, Dr Jordan had become her haven and safe place to just release the stress.

Karen dressed the part as expected of her for the Sunday luncheon. She had spoken to JJ about his anger and reminded him he was not to embarrass his father at the luncheon. As soon as it came out her mouth, she recognized that she sounded like her mother and she hated that thought. With that realization, she took JJ by the hand and walked him into his room. She closed his door behind them. They sat down on the bed. "Sweetheart, I want to share something with you, but it must be just our secret." JJ could read the seriousness on his mother's face. He nodded his head. She continued, "I am so grateful to you. You made me look at myself and my neglect in taking responsibility for how your father treats me. I'm ashamed that that has been the example I have set for you."

JJ looked at her through saddened eyes. "Mom, it isn't your fault. He's a bully."

"Baby, it is my fault too for allowing him to do that to me. So, here is my secret between only you and me. I am seeing a counselor who is showing me how to be stronger and not let myself be a victim of him or…" She hesitated as she thought of the rape. "Or anyone. So, I don't want you to worry about me because I am getting stronger every day." She smiled at him reassuringly.

"Mom, can't you, me, and Mark just move out? And get away from him. He gets worse all the time and I'm afraid he might hurt you; I mean not with just words."

Karen could cry with happiness hearing that JJ wanted to leave with her. Measuring her words very carefully, she said, "That is the second part of our secret. I am working on that too. That is why it must be a secret, even from Mark, because I don't know how he would feel about moving. and he might say something to your dad. Your dad could stop us. Until I can get us the money to do this, no one, not even Grandma and Grandpa, must know."

"They think everything Dad does is right anyway."

*Out of the mouth of babes.* "Knowing all this now, can you try not to be so angry with your dad now that we have a plan?"

JJ was so excited about the plan and with wide eyes of enthusiasm said, "Mom, you can count on me!"

His eyes lit up and she could see him connecting the dots. "That's why you got a job right? Mom, I'm proud of you."

Her heart melted and she took her mature little man into her arms and held him tight. Jack's voice came from downstairs. "It's time to go, everyone, get down here."

Karen played the trophy wife as expected of her. She smiled and made small talk with friends she no longer had or wanted. Her mother looked at her son-in-law with such pride it suddenly became clear to Karen that he had become her mother's substitute for Mathew.

After lunch, Jack took the podium for his speech and request for donations for his campaign. He was in his element as he bragged about how he had done so much for the city of Tucson and welcomed suggestions from citizens on to his website. Karen kept the plastered smile on her face throughout his speech. Her face hurt as she kept it through the family photo shoot of Jack, herself, and the boys. More photos were taken with her parents; it seemed to go on forever.

It had been a very long day only to be told by her mother that she would be required to attend other campaign required functions. How much was her parents giving, she wondered? She could be free from all of them for what her parents were probably giving him for his campaign.

## Ann

Dr Stein's therapy required a group session every other week. Ann did not use that in her own practice and felt a little uncomfortable the first time she attended. At the second group session, Ann began to understand its benefits. The participants were more inclined to open up with each other as they recognized they were struggling with similar issues. The process also gave the participants confidence as they shared suggestions and found strengths. The group of five included four women and a man. Dr Stein asked the group if they would be interested in participating in a self-defense class, pointing out how important it is for rape victims to feel more empowered. Ann thought about the man who had attacked her. He was large and powerful. She could not picture herself being able to defend herself, but she did grab his hair at the scalp instinctively at the moment the adrenaline kicked in. She felt good about that.

A petite woman named Nancy was the first to point out the same concern. "The man that attacked me was a big guy. I don't think a class like that would have helped me."

Marty Stein acknowledged her concern and pointed out, "This class does not require you to have physical power. The instructor of this class teaches you how to react instinctively and go after vulnerable parts of a person's body. Gouging eyes, knees to the groin, stepping hard on the instep, and so on, hopefully enabling you to *escape* the attacker." Marty could see a couple women cringe at these descriptions of defense. "I can see that you may be uncertain if you could do these things to another person. Under normal circumstances you probably couldn't, but as you all have experienced first-hand, rape is not normal." Marty waited a few seconds for that to sink in and then added, "When you each relive that attack in your mind, I'm pretty sure you feel helpless. Part of that feeling is, what should I have done? It's like a video played over and over in your mind, am I right?" Everyone, including Ann, nodded. Marty continued, "With these types of skills comes more confidence and confidence gives us power."

After class, Ann signed up for the self-defense class and returned to the office for her scheduled session with Meg. She had a few minutes to eat her lunch at her desk and look over her notes before Meg arrived. She hoped that Meg was coping a little better, but that was obviously not the case when she walked through the door. Meg's physical appearance had not improved. She once again had not made an attempt to put on makeup or fix her hair. Ann was concerned that her depression was worsening. Her body dropped limply into the easy chair.

Ann chose not to comment about her concerns and asked, "Meg, how was your week?"

It was an effort for Meg to respond as she slowly made eye contact. "Dr Weise, I'm not sure how much more I can take. Rick lost his job and had to move in with me. He is trashing my place and I sure not sure I can handle him. He made a scene at Mom's assisted living facility again. If that isn't enough my car broke down. I really needed to see you today, so Randy brought me."

Ann smiled at her. "Well, I'm glad he did. How did Rick lose his job and what does he do?"

"He's a mechanic." She shook her head. "He has been warned a few times to watch his language around customers. He doesn't listen and when he was told that a customer complained, he said he knew who it was, and he'd shut her up for good." Meg threw her hands up in exasperation. "He kept talking about the woman who got him fired. He said he had killed a lady hiker and he could do the same to this one.”

“Do you believe he did kill a hiker?”

Meg started to cry softly. “I believe he could. I don’t know if he was just bragging or not.”

“What does Randy think? Did they discuss it, or was it just said in passing?”

Meg ignored the reference to Randy and said, “It’s not the first time Rick said he killed someone. He said he killed that weather girl on television. The one that was on the news for a while.”

Ann’s heart started to race. *My God, could her brother really be the one that killed Addie?* Ann struggled to keep a poker face. “Did he say why he killed her?”

“He said she needed to die because she could get him in trouble. I’m thinking she was another customer who complained to his boss.”

Ann’s head was spinning with questions. *Did he know her? Was it a random break-in to her apartment? Perhaps he had dated Addie and the hiker?* She knew she needed to slow down and not get ahead of herself or upset her. “Meg, you had said Rick was in the hospital recovering from injuries from a fight. When was he released?”

Meg could see where Ann’s question was leading, she nodded and said, “I thought about that. He was released about seven months before that news lady was killed. I remembered because it was around the same time he was living back home with Mom, and we knew we had to get her out of the house away from him. That's when we put her in assisted living. So yeah, he was out around that time. God, I pray he is just bragging about killing two women."

Ann ventured cautiously, she asked, "Did you or Randy know if Rick was seeing anyone?"

Meg slowly shook her head and said, "He never mentioned anyone. Oh my! Do you think he might have been dating these women for real before he...?" Meg stopped herself from finishing her sentence.

Ann knew she had to stop obsessing about her own experience and deal with Meg's needs. "Meg we really don't know if he did in fact do what he said. We aren't sure Rick has really killed people or if it's all in his head." Ann didn't want to cause any more anxiety for her, so she switched gears and asked, "How is Randy doing?"

Meg became agitated. "Dr Weise, we keep telling Rick we cannot keep getting him out of trouble and that he can't keep doing terrible things. If he has, what can we do anyway?"

"Meg, Rick needs to get counseling. Has he ever been in the military or diagnosed with post traumatic syndrome?"

Meg looked embarrassed and weary. "He got a dishonorable discharge from the army for beating on another solider."

Ann's heart went out to Meg. "I know this is difficult. Let me do some research with the VA and perhaps find him someone to see for his anger issues."

"That is very nice of you, Dr Weise. I just don't think Randy and I could get him to go."

Ann smiled reassuringly. "One step at a time, let me look into it and then we can go from there. Let's talk a little bit about you. How is your job at the dentist office going?"

Meg seemed to be relieved to regroup her thoughts away from her brothers. "I must admit, it's been difficult getting up to go to work the last few weeks. I seem to be exhausted all the time. Sometimes just taking a shower and getting dressed is overwhelming. All I want to do is sleep. Thank goodness my boss is a great guy. At the last minute, I'm taking a few days of my vacation time and I'm going to rent a car while mine is in the shop. I'm going to drive up to Pinetop tomorrow, only sleep, eat, and read novels for a few days." Her face went from contented, to sad. "Maybe someday I can have a normal life. I'd like to date and meet a nice man and settle down. I don't see that in my future." This was said as a preamble before returning to her ongoing reality. "I just feel guilty and hope Randy is around to keep Rick in line while I'm away. I need to get away for a break."

Ann was pleased to hear Meg was planning some time to herself. "I think that is an excellent idea. Exhaustion, the need to sleep excessively, are very common signs of depression. A few days to yourself will be a healthy change. If it isn't enough for you, we may need to discuss some medication. It would be a small dosage just to help take the edge off your depression. It's important not to let depression interfere with your daily life and routine."

Meg seemed agreeable to the suggestion. She ran her hand over her unruly hair. "I'm not eating well and I'm not unaware of how I look lately."

Ann was pleased she was conscious of these other symptoms. "That is all part of the depression and I'm glad that you recognize it as such. Would you like me to write you a prescription now? It takes a little while for it to build up in your system." Meg agreed and Ann wrote it out and handed it to her. Ann smiled and discreetly looked at the time. "I am a little jealous of your time away. I think I can use a little of that myself. Well, our time is up for today."

Ann patted Meg's back as she stepped into the reception area to leave. A man stood up as they closed Ann's door behind them. Meg smiled and said, "Dr Weise, this is my brother Randy."

Ann reached for the back of an empty chair to steady herself. She was looking into the face of the man that attacked her. Ann thought she might faint or vomit. The room spun briefly before she could regain control. He smiled and put his hand out to shake hers. She slowly took his hand reaching out to her. This was Rick's twin brother! A much cleaned up version of his brother with a warm smile. She held onto the chair paralyzed, even after they left. An instant sweat had dampened her blouse and dripped down between her breasts. Peggy looked up from her desk. "Dr Weise, are you okay? You look as white as a sheet."

# CHAPTER 7
## Karen

JJ's angry behavior had improved significantly since Karen shared her secret with him. Karen was enjoying her job and she had to deal less and less with Jack now that he was busy with both work and his campaign. Her therapy was going well with Dr Jordan.

Jamie found activities that the boys could share. Karen looked forward to coming home to happy kids. Karen followed the laughter into the kitchen, where Jamie and the boys were cooking together. Jamie was asking Mark to measure out sixteen ounces of chicken stock. "How many ounces are in one cup?" she asked Mark.

Mark looked at Jamie proudly. "Eight. So, I need two of them, right?"

Jamie rustled his hair. "Good job."

Karen hadn't yet been noticed so she announced, "Well, I am impressed. So, can I expect breakfast in bed tomorrow?"

They looked up from their cooking and smiled. "Hi, Mom," came from them both.

"I see all is going well in here. I'm going to change out of these clothes. I'll be right down." Karen got to the top step when her phone rang. She took it from her pocket and continued into her bedroom. "Hello."

"Hello, Karen. This is Ann Weise." Ann had spent the rest of the day debating what to do. She knew she could not keep today's discovery to herself. Randy's twin brother was alive and possibly had been the one that killed Addie. As nonchalant as she could pull off, she said, "I realize this is a bit unorthodox, but I wonder if we could meet, say for lunch tomorrow?"

Karen was pleasantly surprised to hear her voice. "I have my appointment with Dr Jordan late tomorrow afternoon. How about dinner after?"

"That will work for me as well. At what time and where would like to meet?"

Time and place were agreed upon.

The following day, Karen entered the restaurant five minutes early but spotted Ann at a back table. She smiled at Ann and placed her purse on the chair next to her and sat down. Ann didn't want to jump in with the shocking news. "I'm so glad you could make it. I ordered a drink; would you like one while we look over the menu?"

"That sounds lovely. It's been a long day." Ann waved at the waiter, who came over and Karen's drink was ordered. They studied the menu for a few minutes and placed their orders.

Ann chuckled, "Well… you know what I do. What about you? Where do you work?"

They ate their meals while conversation continued easily between them as they got to know a little more about each other's lives. Ann didn't want to ruin the evening by jumping into the shocking news that Rick was still alive, so she started off slowly. "When I first saw you in my office, I had such mixed emotions. I felt such a deep connection, but I was afraid to overstep any boundaries. I was reluctant to talk to you because of the circumstances, you know professionally." Ann took a deep breath, letting it out slowly. "As I said last night this meeting is unorthodox but I'm glad we are getting to know each other."

Karen sensed something was upsetting Ann. She placed her hand over Ann's in a comforting way. "Ann, what is it? Why did you change your mind?"

"I have information I have to share with you about that night in the garage." She swallowed hard with emotion. Having not been prepared for what happened in the office yesterday, Ann knew Karen was in for a shock as well. There was no easy way to soften the blow. She prefaced the news with, "Again because of professional reasons, I can't tell you how this has come to my attention." She looked deeply into Karen's questioning eyes. "That horrible man did not die that night. He survived and I'm afraid he might be the one who murdered Addie Carson. I have been up all night, thinking about this. If he did, there may be a chance he could be looking for us too."

The color had drained from Karen's face, and her hand shook slightly as she picked up her drink and took a sip, as her mouth had gone dry. Karen was visibly shaken. Her neck and face instantly turned splotchy red. Ann reached across the table and took her hand. Her palm was sweaty. The silence remained between them as Ann allowed Karen to digest this information. Karen was just beginning to feel she had control of where her life was going and once again her life changed in an instant. She squeezed Ann's hand and finally, Karen spoke. "Ann, what are we going to do?" This was said calmly but with a frightened look.

"I just found out yesterday and I knew I had to tell you right away. To answer your question, I don't know. I just know we have to be very aware of our surroundings and protect ourselves until we figure this out."

Karen nodded, "Agreed." She went on to confess, "I never went to the police, did you?"

Ann sighed, "No. I drove by the place about a week later. It was burned down to the ground. I wondered if Addie came back and set it on fire, thinking she'd make sure he was dead. Now I wonder if he burned it down to get rid of the evidence."

Never moving her eyes from Ann's stare. Karen said, "I know you said you can't share everything about what you have learned, but can you tell me the name of the man that did this to us?"

"Rick." No last name was given to her. "I saw his twin brother in my reception room."

As shivers traveled down Karen's back, she said, "That had to have been terrifying!" She had to know, and she asked Ann directly, "Does Dr Jordan know about both of us being there that night?"

Ann understood immediately and wanted to reassure her. "I have never discussed you with her. She does know about that night in terms of what happened to me, and that there were other women in that warehouse."

Karen stated matter-of-factly, "Well, she does now. Just today I finally opened up to her about that night without mentioning you. Up until today's session, she and I have been dealing with just my situation at home. I am hoping to leave my husband and take my two boys to California. This news has made me rethink…" Ann watched as Karen seemed to switched thoughts in her mind and then continued, "My husband has influence in town and unfortunately my parents will support him and not me when I leave with my boys. With the news you just gave me, now I also have to be concerned about my kids' safety. My brother lives in California and maybe I shouldn't wait any longer, just take the boys and go." She took a deep breath. "My husband is running for office and in the next few days there will be publicity posters and fliers all over town with our family pictures. That could lead this Rick, right to me and my family.

I'm so conflicted. I can't leave town and let you deal with this madman by yourself, but…"

Ann interrupted her, "No! No, you have to think of the boys first. Go to your brother's. Leave before the campaign fliers go out!"

Almost pleading, Karen said, "Now that I've opened up to Dr Jordan, you have to tell her about this man being alive. You need someone to help you!"

"I promise I will. As I shared with you earlier, Kate is my best friend, and Nicky is my life support. I will be okay. I'll figure out what to do, but right now you have to leave for California as soon as you can. How about you? You will be leaving Kate. Have you any emotional support? You still need to be able to talk through all the trauma."

"My brother, he knows too. He's amazing. I'll be fine."

Ann nervously ran her hand through her hair and said, "Just because I'm a therapist doesn't mean I have answers. You have dealt more proactively about healing from this than I have. I am struggling with how this has affected me and my life. I find it overwhelming sometimes."

It was if Ann had read her mind, she said, "Yes! oh God yes! How could anyone understand unless they were there that night? You can tell them, but there is no way for them to understand what facing death can be like… what we survived."

Tears pooled in both women's eyes. Once again there was that instant connection to the experience they shared and had changed their lives forever. Ann finally felt she could breathe, knowing she was not alone; Karen was the only other person who truly understood. A little ashamed, Ann lowered her head and said, "You know Karen, as much as Nicky and Kate have been so supportive, there is no way they could understand what day to day life has been for me since that night. It haunts me, it makes me see normal everyday events as fearful. I keep so much of it to myself because I don't want it to change my relationships with them. Sometimes I cling so strongly to wanting normalcy back in my live, that I'm afraid to move forward."

Karen looked so sad. She felt so much of what Ann was expressing. Karen reached across the table and gently stroked Ann's face and said, "Other than my brother and my grandmother, I have never had relationships I was fearful of losing. Ironically, it took that night to make me see I wanted to be free from what my life is right now. I want a life like you have described to me this evening. We both have experienced how fleeting life can be, I'm not wasting a second chance to change my life. You have what is important in your life, don't let that monster paralyze you from moving on with it."

Ann looked into Karen's eyes. She smiled broadly and said, "You could be the therapist I always wanted to be."

Karen chuckled. "You know exactly who you are, I'm on a journey to find out who I am."

The smile remained on Ann's face. "Thank you for reminding me. It's very comforting to know we also have each other for support. That means the world to me." They nodded simultaneously. Ann didn't want Karen to hesitate for a minute with her decision to go to California with her boys. She continued with, "I'll let Kate know you will be leaving town and won't be at your next appointment. We both are going to be okay." They exchanged emails and hugs and agreed to check in with each other often.

## Ann

Ann was so relieved she had asked Karen to meet her. Now at least Karen and her boys will be safe. She left the restaurant and as she drove home, she was acutely aware of her surroundings. She looked in ever car window that passed her. She made sure the car behind her wasn't following. By the time she got home her hands were shaking. She let herself into the house and locked the door behind her.

It was Friday night. Nicky was at the hospital and Ann felt vulnerable. She paced a few minutes trying to calm herself. *He doesn't know I'm his sister's psychiatrist. He is still, probably, unaware where I work or live. Think, think, don't panic.* Ann poured herself a glass of wine and sat down on the couch to think. *I have to know more about Rick and how he thinks. I have to get into his head.* Coco climbed into her lap and settled in for some petting. Ann scratched behind her ears and she purred contently. She smiled down at her and said, "Karen is right, I can't let him paralyze me." She put her wine down on the end table and opened her laptop. She started reading research journals and articles on psychosis. As she read, course studies she had not used in her practice began to resurface. Coco insistently rubbed up against her arm. Ann stroked her silky fur, "I'm sorry, Miss Coco, I forgot to get you your dinner." Ann took a break to feed the cat and herself.

Nicky was gently shaking Ann awake. She had worked a double shift and found Ann sleeping against the couch cushions, her black screened laptop open and off to the side. "Hey, baby, you must have been here all night. It's five in the morning. Come with me to bed." Nicky always slept better if Ann was curled up against her.

Ann blinked and pushed away the images she had been reading about and personally experienced with Rick's rage. Ann took Nicky's hand and followed her into the bedroom. She could see that Nicky was exhausted and that she needed sleep. They took off their clothes and climbed into bed. "Nicky, after we sleep, let's meet Kate for dinner tonight."

Nicky was already spooned into Ann's body and almost out for the count. She grunted an "Okay". Ann remained next to her, now wide awake. She waited until

Nicky was in a deep, needed sleep before slipping out of bed. Ann reached for her silk robe at the foot of the bed and tied the sash around her. She made herself a cup of coffee and returned to her research.

It was a little after ten. Ann knew Kate was an early riser. She texted her and got a response immediately that it was Kate's turn to cook and dinner was at six. Ann had signed up for the self-defense class and the first class was at eleven-thirty. She left a note for Nicky and headed out.

Ann entered the gym at Sahuaro High School. Marty was talking to a few women standing around mats scattered on the gym floor. Ann joined them and was welcomed to the class. A few minutes passed and a muscular looking man walked in and started to rearrange the mats. He and Marty waved at each other. It was exactly eleven-thirty when he announced class was about to start. After Marty thanked the three women who came, Ann being one of the three, she introduced Scott.

Ann was surprised that Marty was the instructor for their class and Scott was there to act as the attacker. In the following thirty minutes it was clear Marty could defend herself. She demonstrated how to respond to attacks from all angles. The next hour each woman took turns at defending themselves from Scott's controlled attacks. The women practiced the movements trying to react without hesitation. These were alien, and not instinctive moves for most women. Women generally did not relate to being physically aggressive. Attackers counted on that fact. At the end of class, the women were surprised that they actually had skills that might give them time to escape an attacker. Marty reminded the women that it was one thing to have these tools in a controlled environment. It was quite another thing in a real situation. These skills had to be practiced over and over until they became instant responses. Hesitation was their enemy as well as the attacker. Ann's confidence took a small step forward. She knew she had a long way to go with the knowledge that he was still out there possibly looking for her, and could once again be lurking in shadows, but this session gave her the much-needed beginnings of a sense of empowerment.

Nicky and Ann arrived at Kate's for dinner. Brad was in the kitchen helping by setting the table. So much had happened in the last two days that Ann thoughts distracted her from the conversation ongoing by the others. She was trying to put together the newest puzzle pieces in her mind. Nicky had been discussing a possible get-away for the four of them. Ann was lost in conversations she had with Meg about her brothers. Ann interrupted the ongoing discussion, "Brad, remember you had mentioned a man that had been stabbed multiple times over a year ago and survived. You saw him in the emergency room a few weeks ago. Could you describe him?"

After exchanging confused looks with Kate and Nicky over Ann's random question, he said, "Yeah." He closed his eyes briefly to bring the man back to mind. "He was about six-foot-four or so. He had nondescript brown hair and green eyes. No facial hair. He was muscular." Brad hesitated while he continued to recall more details.

Ann asked, "Did he have any tattoos or piercings?"

Brads eyebrows elevated in remembering. "Yes. He had a cross on his inner arm. I think it was the left. I don't think he had any piercings."

Ann did not look shocked with the confirmation that Rick was indeed still alive. She stated firmly, "The tattoo is on his left arm." She began to feel somehow empowered knowing this revelation. Without further explanation for the moment, she stated emphatically, "That was the man that attacked us in the warehouse."

Everyone's forks were held in suspension as they stared at Ann. Finally, Kate spoke in a shaky voice, "Does this have anything to do with Karen?"

Nicky, now totally confused and shocked, gestured with palms up. "Who is Karen?"

Kate offered an explanation. "She is a patient of mine that Ann sent to me for therapy. Did she see him again?"

Ann put her fork down. "No, I did. He is the brother of a patient of mine. Actually, I saw his twin. They look so much alike it was very startling. Both her twins are alive."

Nicky shook her head in confusion. "So, what the fuck has this got to do with this Karen woman?"

Kate leaving Nicky's question hanging addressed everyone at the table,

"At our last session, she told me about that night she was raped. She didn't mention Ann by name, but she didn't have to."

Ann continued to explain what she had figured out. "My patient told me she was concerned that her brother might have been the man who killed Addie Carson. She was the other woman in the warehouse who escaped that night."

Brad had now made the final connection. "Oh my god! He may be looking for you and this *Karen* woman!"

Nicky looked very frightened and grabbed Ann's arm. "Honey, we have to go to the police. Right away."

Ann patted Nicky's hand. With calmly logic she said, "With what, honey? We have no proof of anything. The warehouse is burned to the ground. Addie's murder is still a mystery and seems like it's been a closed case for months now. They can't just drag a man in with just a suspicion. We didn't report the rape. There is nothing for them to investigate." Ann looked at Nicky's worried face. She kissed her cheek. "Nick, my patient's information is privileged between me and her. I can't divulge private conversations."

Nicky's concern turned to fear as tears accumulated in her eyes. "Well, we have to do something. We can't sit idly by while he may be out there looking for you."

Kate pushed her chair back and came around the table to wrap her arms around her two best friends. "The first thing we are going to do is hire a security guard at the office."

Nicky shook her head vigorously in agreement. "Yes, and he has to follow you to the office and follow you home until you are safely inside the house."

Brad agreed and added, "I know a guy who does bodyguard work. He's a good guy and maybe he can help us."

Dinner was abandoned as they took their conversation into the living room, where Nicky curled up with Ann on the couch. Kate's brow wrinkled with concern. "I'm worried about Karen now too."

Ann turned to Nicky. "Honey, I wanted to tell you about this last night, but you could barely keep your eyes open, you were so exhausted." Ann related to them her dinner meeting with Karen. "I told her. Her husband is running for city office and she said campaign signs will soon be posted. They will have her family photos on them." Ann addressed Kate. "Karen won't be back for her session. She plans to take her boys out of town before they are distributed."

Kate nodded. "That explains her message on my answering service this afternoon. I wondered why she cancelled. She was really making progress and I hope this doesn't set her back."

Ann reassured Kate, "In the short time I've known her, she impresses me as a strong confident woman. I would have liked more time to get to know her better as a friend. I'm just thankful she will be out of harm's way and keep her kids safe."

No time was wasted. The next day, Brad returned with his friend's recommendation for a guard for Ann. The following night, Nicky and Ann met with Jerry at the house with Brad and Kate in attendance. They were all wanting to make sure he would be right for the job. It was explained that Ann was in danger. They gave Jerry Rick's description. Jerry was a formidable and intimidating man in appearance. His upper arms and chest could barely be contained in his suit. When he sat down on the couch his thighs stretched the fabric of his pants to its limits. He had a stoic broad face and his thick neck looked like it was cemented to his shoulders. He listened quietly as his job description was outlined. He inquired about an alarm system in both the office and Ann and Nicky's home. Jerry approved of both but recommended adding a few more security features that made them all feel safer. He obviously had experience with this type of work, and Ann felt less frightened by her situation.

Jerry started right away and within the following few days, Ann began to understand how celebrities felt by constantly having a shadow follow them. In her case a large one. Even when she and Kate went to lunch, Jerry sat at another table within the view of the entry.

Meg's appointment was this afternoon and Ann needed to try and get into Rick's head through his sister.

Meg didn't look as rested after her getaway to the mountains. She took a seat today on the couch not the easy chair, her usual choice. She attempted a smile that was not very convincing. "Hi, Dr Weise."

Ann smiled back. "Hi. So, tell me, how was your vacation?"

Meg smiled a little more convincingly. "It was really good. So relaxing and great being able to just get away for a few days. I wish I didn't have to come home." Meg's face instantly changed, showing her stress. Ann remained silent, not wanting to cut off Meg's continuing thoughts that came next. "Then I got home. Right back to it. While I was away, Rick tried to force his way into the facility again, insisting on to see Mom. Sierra Del Sol is a really nice place and I don't want him to get Mom thrown out. They called the cops and he took off. Then he trashed my house."

Ann waited a few seconds to see if Meg had more to say.

"Meg, did he get another job?"

She shook her head. "No, not yet."

Ann asked Meg, "Are you afraid to throw him out? Would he become violent with you?"

Meg's face reddened with embarrassment. She conceded, "I think he would. Once, awhile back, I put a restraining order on him and it only lasted seventy-two hours. When the time was up, he was really angry and beat me up." Ann could certainly relate to that experience with Meg's brother. She could feel the anger building but forced herself to concentrate on Meg. She could see that it was difficult for Meg to tell her this. "Sometimes I just wish I could just pick up and move away and not let him know where I am. I can't do that yet, not while Mom is still alive."

Ann knew that domestic violence was one of the most difficult issues to deal with. Meg was a person who was not yet strong enough to remove herself from the situation. Her fear only fueled a man like Rick giving him all the power and control. The added burden for Meg was to protect her mother from him.

"Tell me more about your mom. Is she aware that Rick has attempted to see her where she is living? Is she afraid of him as well?"

"I haven't told her that Rick has been trying to see her. I think she would be frightened if she knew. She knows she is there for her own safety. Mom has had a rough life. She only knows abuse. First with her own father's abuse, then my father's abuse, and then Rick's. She deserves to be free of it all. She is a kind woman and I just want her to live the rest of her life no longer afraid."

Ann searched Meg's sad face and gently asked, "How about you, Meg? Don't you deserve to be free of it all too? Like you have stated in the past, you want to be in a good relationship and have a family of your own." Ann suddenly felt an overwhelming ache for Meg's fear. Ann realized she, and Meg, shared the same fear from the same man. "I mentioned to you last time we met that I would check with Veteran Affairs about counseling for Rick. Unfortunately, I agree with you that he would probably not agree to go. I have also done some research on my own about Rick's violent behavior patterns from what you have shared with me. Outside of a very carefully controlled environment, he is not going to get the help he needs. His unpredictable outbursts are going to be on-going occurrences with violence. You and Randy know what I'm talking about better than anyone else. You have to understand if he did as he said he did, kill the weather girl and a hiker, that his violence has now escalated into murder." The vision of the dead woman under the tarp flashed into Ann's mind. That had been more than eighteen months ago. "His illness has progressed to possible murder. He is beyond the point where you or Randy can control him. You are in real danger. Given his violence with you and your mother in the past, you may not be safer just because you are his family. For our next visit we need to explore what your needs are going forward. So, talk to Randy and think about possible actions needed to be taken. We will discuss them at our next session."

Ann sat thinking about Meg long after she had left the office. As she started to make her notes, it occurred to her that Meg had not mentioned Randy. She wondered if he had suffered any consequences since Rick had lost his job.

At the end of the workday, Jerry saw Ann home and insisted on checking the house before leaving her for the day. Nicky was doing another double shift, so Ann just made herself a sandwich for her dinner. Since learning that Rick was alive, Ann was acutely aware of her surroundings. She listened more closely to the sounds the house made. The sound of the ice maker in the refrigerator, the whirl of the fan when the air conditioner flipped on. She would lower the television volume on the remote when she heard a noise outside. She became attuned to Coco's sudden moves or perked up cat ears. Just as she did now. She too had heard something. Ann went to the window and looked out to the front yard in time to see the back of a small red car disappear down the street. Coco was already cleaning her fur undisturbed. It was nothing.

The next day she had an easy day of just two sessions. Even so, she found it difficult to concentrate on her patients. Her mind was constantly wandering back to Rick and wondering where he was. She finished her last notes for the day, it was only three o'clock. She took out notes from Meg's last session and read them over again. So much more was needed for her to understand her enemy. She decided it was time to visit Meg's mother at the Sierra Del Sol. Whatever insight she could get about Rick, the more control she would feel.

# CHAPTER 8
## Karen

The hardest part was having to tell Doug there was a family emergency, knowing she wouldn't be coming back to work. She felt terrible leaving the way she did. Immediately after having dinner with Ann, she began planning what she had to do. It was the last week of school for the boys. She told them that since nothing much would be going on academically this week, they were going to start an early summer vacation. She took Mathew and Greg's idea and told the boys their destination was going to be a surprise. She knew she couldn't leave Jamie alone at the house. She confided in Jamie and JJ that they were really leaving Jack. She asked Jamie to join her and the boys. Jamie was excited to go as well. They did not let Mark know about the real reason they were leaving. Karen knew she would need the car when they got to California, so she announced it would be a road trip.

She packed only the essentials for herself and clothes she would need to look for a job. she shipped almost all the boys' clothes ahead to Mathew the day before they were to leave, leaving out only a few outfits to wear for a few days. Jack was so busy with his campaign that he barely took notice when Karen told him she was taking the boys to Disneyland.

Karen and Ann had texted almost daily as they promised. She finally took a sigh of relief as she drove out of Tucson. The timing couldn't have been better. The following day, Jack's campaign signs and fliers were distributed across Tucson.

# Ann

She glanced at her phone as the text coming in from Karen. She was on her way to California. *Thank God*, Ann thought as she passed a sign for Jack's campaign along the road. Ann had stopped for gas and saw a flier at the pay window with Karen and her family smiling faces. It was months before the election and Jack had not wasted any time getting his name and face known.

She pulled into the parking lot of Sierra Del Sol Assisted Living. She looked around at passers-by, making sure she didn't see Rick sitting in a nearby car. She really didn't have a plan for her conversation with Meg's mother. She had to be careful not to disclose her professional relationship with Meg but was not sure how she was going to introduce herself.

She first scanned the lobby for Rick, only a woman and her young son sat on a couch looking at a magazine. She smiled at the receptionist at the desk and asked as casually she could which room Mrs Cross was in. The two phones at the desk were ringing. The receptionist said, "Room twelve," and answered the phone. "Please hold," she said into the phone as she pushed a sign-in sheet toward Ann and picked up the second phone. Ann signed her name and proceeded down the hall to Mrs Cross.

The door was slightly ajar. Ann knocked and peaked around the door. "Mrs Cross, may I come in?" Trish Cross was a lot younger than Ann expected. She was sitting in her easy chair reading. There was a cup of coffee on the end table beside her. Ann estimated her to be in her late fifties. Her hair was streaked with gray; her skin was wrinkled beyond her age, and her smile was kind. She had a trim figure like her daughter and was dressed in a plain flowered blouse and brown pants. Ann smiled back. "Hello, I saw your door was partially open and wondered if we could talk?"

Trish placed her bookmark at the page she had just finished and placed her reading on the table next to her coffee. "That would be nice. It's so kind of you volunteers to come by to visit. It can get very lonely. I'm not big on playing cards but I do enjoy visits. My daughter is busy most of the week with work and I see her only on weekends." Ann was relieved that Trish's assumption was that she was a volunteer and was not about to correct her. "Can I offer you a cup of coffee? I'm afraid I have no creamer but then I drink it black with just a hint of sugar."

Ann smiled and said, "That sounds perfect." Trish motioned to the second hospital type chair. Ann took a seat and watched as Trish stood from her chair and went to the little side bar setup with a coffee maker. It was not far from where she had been sitting, but Ann could see that she was dragging her right leg. Ann started to rise. "Please, let me get that."

Trish waved dismissingly. "No, I'm very capable of doing this on my own. Thank you."

Ann suspected that that the injury was not a recent one. "Mrs Cross, have you injured yourself?"

"Please call me Trish. No. I slipped many years ago in my kitchen and broke my thigh bone. It never healed well." Ann knew enough to know that a bone that large was not easily broken by a slip and if it had been done years before, she was still young enough to heal. She suspected it was from a brutal kick, either from her husband or her son. Nicky had described enough abuse injuries to her to make that assumption.

"I'm sorry to hear that. You mentioned your daughter visits on the weekend, you must look forward to that? Do you have other children as well?"

Trish returned and placed Ann's coffee on the end table. "Just my twins."

"Oh, are the twins also in town?"

"Oh no. My daughter and her twin brother. They are my only children."

It took everything Ann had not to show the shudder that ran through her. She calmed herself the best she could. With a catch in her voice, she inquired, Ann needed to be absolutely sure she had heard correctly. "How nice, what are your *two* children's names?"

"My sweet girl is Megan, Meg for short, and her twin is Rick."

Ann's hand began to shake as she struggled to place the cup on the end table without spilling the coffee. *Then who is Randy? What is going on?* She returned her hands to her lap. "Tell me about your twins, are they close?"

Trish nodded. "Meg is a doll. She has always looked after Rick even as a child. He was a handful." She shook her head as if recalling those days. "That boy was always in trouble and Meg was there to get him back on track." She leaned forward and in a conspiratorial whisper she said, "He can't come to visit me here any more. He has a temper and he was rude to the staff."

"I'm sorry to hear that." Ann needed more, "Do you miss his visits?"

Trish's face turned a little red. "No. I don't want to be embarrassed, and I don't want them to kick me out of here. I like this place; it's quiet, *safe* and the people are nice."

Ann took a risk in her questioning. "Has Rick been violent in the past?"

Trish's face instantly showed her stress. "He got thrown out of the army because of it. I worry all the time. I'm so scared that he might lose his temper and hurt my Meg."

Ann could see that Trish needed to talk and release some of her fears. It was also an opportunity to hear Trish's insights about Rick. "Do you think he might go get some help controlling his anger issues."

Mrs Cross shook her head strongly, "Oh no, he's just like his father. My husband was …"

She stopped. Ann didn't need to push her about her husband. She had heard Meg describe him during their sessions. "Trish, has he hurt Meg before?"

Ann could see that the question made Trish very uncomfortable. She was nervously rubbing at the seam of her pant leg. Ann did not expect Trish's confession. "I'm ashamed. I'm not a good mother. I could never control Rick. Poor Meg had to be his mother. He only listens to her. I guess twins are very protective of each other. At least mine always have been. There is a strong bond there, but I should not have let Meg deal with Rick by herself, that's not fair. Rick was always a sickly kid. He always got colds and he even got the chicken pox twice. He has all kinds of food allergies and has reactions to things. I couldn't even use the EpiPen. Meg had to do it. She did everything for him. I must confess I have been afraid of Rick ever since he was little. He is just like his father."

Ann was about to comment further when they were interrupted with a knock at the door. They both looked up at the nurse entering with Trish's dinner tray. "Mrs Cross, they said you wanted an early dinner in your room."

Ann rose from her chair. "Well, it has been nice visiting with you. I'll let you get to your meal before it gets cold."

Trish removed her book, placing it in her lap to make room for her dinner tray. "It was so nice talking with you. Please come back and visit soon."

Ann smiled and took her leave. As she made her way through the reception area, she realized Meg's mother had never even asked her name. She got in her car and not wanting to linger at the possibility of Rick, *not an imaginary Randy,* being nearby. She headed back to the office her head was swimming with this frightening new information. That man in her office picking up Meg, was her *only brother… and my rapist. He knows where I am!*

Ann entered her office and sat behind her desk. *Now what?* she thought.

*Now what* didn't take long at all. Jerry knocked on Ann's office door and entered before she could respond. Her bodyguard Jerry did not look happy, but then again, Ann had never seen a smile on his intimidatingly stern face. He didn't wait for her to acknowledge him and said, "You broke the rules. You are not to leave the office or your home without me knowing." A further accusation followed. "You did not text me. I need to know where you are at all times."

Ann felt like she was five again and had run into the street in her father's presence. "Jerry, I'm sorry, I had a lot on my mind and forgot to text you. I had to go over—"

Jerry didn't wait to hear her explanation. "I went by the house to check if you went home." His voice softened slightly before telling her, "Listen, things have gotten serious. Your cat was stabbed and left on the porch. I'm sorry. There was a note left on the body. It said '*You're next*'. Jerry watched Ann's face turn to shock. He wasn't sure if her frightful response was to her cat or to the note. He continued with the news a little more gently. "Look, I didn't mean to be so blunt, but you can't be off on your own, I took some pictures before I buried her. You don't have to see them, but we might need them for the police at some point. I have the note in a plastic bag for possible DNA evidence. He got in through the screened-in patio where the cat door is. I have pictures of that as well." He only showed her a picture on his phone of the slashed screen where Coco's kitty litter box was kept.

She couldn't believe that Coco had been killed so viciously. A tear slid down her cheek thinking how sweet and loving she had been. Nicky would be devastated. They had sweet Coco since she was a kitten. She was like their child. Ann finally found her voice and told him where she had been and the news that there was no Randy, just a Rick. Rick Cross. For the time being, Jerry insisted on staying in Ann and Nicky's guest room. They went to his place to pack a few things Jerry would need. They then drove to Nicky and Ann's house where he settled into his temporary room. Ann took a shower where she could privately cry for Coco and try and absorb the magnitude of events that had taken place.

# Karen

It was such a relief being out of Tucson. Karen decided to go to Disneyland before heading up to Mathew in San Francisco. Jamie and the boys were having a great time. For now, Jack was still paying Jamie's salary until he figured out that they were not coming back. She texted daily to Ann, letting her know how she was doing and asking about Ann's safety.

Mathew's place was much too small for her, Jamie, and the boys, so he got them a furnished apartment not too far from their apartment. He was unable to get a place month to month, so he signed a six-month lease under his Greg's name so that Jack would hopefully not track Karen. The apartment had been painted and was now just waiting for them to arrive from Disneyland. He realized rents would be much too high in the city, but for now he wanted them close by. It had been years since he had seen JJ and Mark. He was looking forward to getting to know his nephews and having a real family for Greg and himself.

It had been a hot and long day at Disneyland. They stopped at an inexpensive restaurant for some dinner before heading back to the hotel for the night. One more day at the park and then on to San Francisco. They were cooling off with cold drinks and waiting for their dinners when Karen's phone pinged. It was a text from her mother, telling her to call as soon as possible. Karen's first thought was she was being summoned to attend some fund raiser for Jack. With renewed confidence she thought, *with a resounding no, that will be quickly put to rest.* She excused herself and made the call from the restaurant lobby. Her mother picked up right away. Without a hello, her mother asked, "Are you at Disneyland yet?"

There was an urgency in her mother's voice. Karen replied, "Yes, why?"

Her mother stated bluntly, "Jack's life has been threatened. I guess now that he is in politics, things like this are going to happen. We think you need to delay coming back. It's best you and the boys aren't here until we can set up some security for the family first."

A little taken aback she asked, "What exactly happened?"

"Some sicko left a dead stabbed animal on your porch and left a note saying '*You are next*' on it. What is wrong with these sick people anyway?"

Karen doubted it was meant for Jack. *That madman has tracked us down fast. God, I hope Ann is all right. I'll call her right away.* "Mother, have Jack transfer some money into my checking account to hold me over."

Without asking about her and the boys' trip, her mother said, "We will be in touch" and hung up.

Karen was not feeling guilty that this extra money transfer was being sent on false pretenses. Then Ann jumped to mind. She immediately texted Ann what she had just heard from her mother. As she was heading back to the table, a text from Ann arrived. It said, "Our house, our cat too. Please call, I need to talk to you. Are you and the boys okay?" Karen returned to the table and saw that their dinners had been served. She took a mouthful of her food and announced she needed to make a call and would be right back. Karen and Ann only spoke a few minutes, enough time for Ann to tell her that the rapist was named Rick and that there was no twin brother. Karen was very upset for Ann and pleaded with her to be careful even with a bodyguard near her. Ann promised and after asking about the boys and their trip, said they would talk soon. The closeness they had formed was a comfort to each other. Karen felt Ann was like having a sister.

## Ann

Meg entered the office for her session with Ann, taking a seat on the chair facing Ann's desk. There was darkening around her eyes and she looked tired. Her hair was combed but it hadn't been washed. Her shoulders slumped as she took her seat.

Ann knew that Jerry was on the premises. Since the incident with Coco, he hadn't left her alone. Just having Meg in her office made her heart beat faster, knowing

Rick could be close by. She stood up and went to the window overlooking the parking lot where Meg's red mini car was parked. She didn't see Rick in the car. She casually mentioned, "It looks like it's still pretty hot out," as she scanned the area looking for Rick. She only saw a woman leaving the building. She returned to her easy chair facing Meg.

"Yeah. It's a hot one all right."

Reassured that Rick was not on the premises, she gave Meg her best smile and asked, "So, Meg, how was your week? Is Rick still staying with you?"

Meg sighed. "Yes. It's time he finds another job and a place of his own. He's out looking, but he is so unsettled lately. He paces and stares off into space the way he does. I just pray he's not out there getting into trouble or hurting someone."

Now knowing that Meg only had her twin brother, Ann eased into the next conversation. She was not sure if Meg was delusional or purposely misleading her that Randy did not exist. "Perhaps Randy could take him in for a while to give you a rest? Were you two able to discuss options like we discussed at our last session?"

Meg looked at Ann almost pleadingly. "Randy has not been around for a while. He usually shows up just when I need him. He just hasn't been there for me lately."

Ann sensed an underlining stress and meaning to Meg's statement. "Tell me about Randy and how he helps you."

"He is kind and thoughtful. He is no trouble and he is calm and easy to talk to."

Ann ventured a little deeper. "He sounds like Rick's opposite."

Meg nodded thoughtfully. "You're right. I wish Randy showed up more."

*We are getting close, tread carefully.* Non-threatening, Ann commented, "You know, it's almost like your own experience of Jekyll and Hyde." Silently while Meg mulled that analogy around in her head, Ann waited. When sufficient time for a response passed, she continued. "People are interesting, and I think sometimes there are different personalities in each of us. Some stronger and much more pronounced than others. I'm sure it's got to be hard seeing that scary side more in *your twin* when you feel so connected and protective of him."

Meg did not seem threatened or surprised by Ann's comment. She did not respond in a frightened way that Ann acknowledged the fact of *her* twin. She ventured carefully. "Rick seems to be present much more frequently, why do you think that is?"

A tear dropped on Meg's cheek followed by more. It was a soundless, short, and a defeated cry, giving away to a calm response. She wiped away the last of the tears and said, "Because I can't kill him, and Rick has totally taken his place now. There is no longer a trace of Randy."

Ann had to know, and she asked as gently as possible, "Did you always know that Rick and Randy were the same brother?"

Meg showed no shame or remorse. "I always saw a bit of Randy in Rick. He was trying so hard to come out when he was a kid. I have been able to show him Randy most of our lives when no one else could. Back then, the good was still trying so hard to come out." Suddenly she looked defeated as her shoulders dropped in frustration. "Over the last year, Randy was rarely there any more. I could see that only Rick was left. Last month he told me that he had killed Randy and I knew, as much as I wanted, he wasn't coming back, no matter how much I tried to point Randy out."

Ann was relieved knowing Meg was aware that Randy wasn't real. Meg needed to explore her present reality a little clearer. "Meg, because you are Rick's twin, you always felt that bond and needed to protect him, am I right?"

Meg's earnest face looked directly at Ann. "Of course. He is my twin brother. I have always been the one who could reach him when Randy wasn't there for him to connect to."

Ann began to understand more clearly. "So, up until recently, did Rick believe Randy was inside of him?"

"Yes. Since he was a child, I would refer to him as Randy when he was kind and Rick when he was… well, you know."

Ann nodded in understanding. "So, *you* knew all along there was only one brother, correct?"

"Yes, but I could control his bad behavior by talking to him as Randy." Meg shook her head, once again defeated. "He killed Randy and now I can no longer control him."

Ann acknowledged her feeling of defeat and at that moment, she felt it as strongly as Meg. "I understand. It must feel as if this whole situation is out of control for you now." *I get it, because I too am not in control of your brother. Ann… regroup.* She had to sound coherent and strong for Meg. "Remember we talked in earlier sessions, that you have never been responsible for Rick's behavior. I understand he is your twin, but you have your own life to live. Thankfully for you, your mother is safe." She needed Meg like herself to find safety. Ann hesitated before continuing, and then she stated, "Meg, you are in real danger. Rick is a volatile threat to you and others. Rick is no longer able to get in touch with his kinder self. He has indeed killed Randy off in his disturbed mind." Ann wanted so much to tell Meg what her brother has done and what he is trying to do now to both herself and Karen, but of course she couldn't. Their session time had gone over, but Ann needed to make Meg understand the seriousness of her situation. "I want you to think about what I just said." Thinking of Karen, Ann said almost in desperation, "Perhaps you can take your mother and both of you can relocate without Rick knowing where." The minute those words left her mouth, she knew she had spoken unprofessionally. She covered her error by saying, "Our time is up for today. We will talk about possible options *you* might come up with in next week's session."

After Meg left her office, Ann sat at her desk thinking. *How could I suggest Meg leave town when she knew Meg had a breakthrough and needed therapy now more than ever.* Ann was angry with herself for her actions when she herself couldn't keep Rick out of her life.

## Karen

The boys were busy with their iPads on the drive up to San Francisco. It gave Karen time to think about how she was going to explain their move to Mark. Mark adored his dad, and Karen was torn about what she should say to him. It would be a half lie to use the threat to Jack's life when she knew now it was really a threat to her. Besides, that would only prolong having to deal with the truth. What was the truth at this point, she wondered? Her leaving Jack was only part of the truth; Rick was the other frightening reality. He was after Ann now too. Karen felt helpless for both of them. *I should leave the boys with Mathew and go back to Tucson to help Ann deal with this. How? What can we do? She has Jerry for her bodyguard, but is he enough? She has a career in Tucson. How can she function under this pressure and fear? What if he comes after Nicky too!*

Her mind was made up. *Once I get the boys and Jamie settled in, I'll go to Ann.*

Mathew's face lit up when his sister and his nephews arrived. He was so relieved to see them. Karen had kept him informed with every changing moment and he couldn't imagine the stress she was under.

The boys could see how their uncle and mother were thrilled to see each other. JJ and Mark watched their mom's elevated energy return the moment they hugged each other. JJ in particular hadn't seen his mom this happy in a very long time. It didn't take him long to understand that Mathew was a really great guy. His father and his uncle couldn't have been more different. Greg was a really nice guy too. JJ understood that they were gay, but he wasn't uncomfortable. He watched his mother's effortless interaction with both men and was comfortable as well. His grandparents and father never talked about Mathew and he now knew why. He was ashamed of them. The first night they had arrived, JJ and Mark shared a bed in a hotel room before moving into their apartment scheduled for the following day. Jamie and his mom shared the other.

Mark whispered to his brother, "Greg and Uncle Mathew kissed in the kitchen when they thought I didn't see them. That makes them gay, right?"

JJ turned to his brother. "There is nothing wrong with that, Mark. They are good guys."

Mark was silent for a moment. "Once Dad said that guys that were gay were sickos. I heard him say that to the other coach Dad works with. He told him that he didn't want that new kid around us, so the other coach told the kid he didn't make the team." Mark hesitated and then finished his thought. "That kid was a really good baseball player."

He and his brother had always been close, and Mark looked up to his brother. JJ could feel the anger his mother asked him to control instantly. He took a deep breath and whispered back to his brother, "Mark, do you know what prejudice means?"

"Yeah, I know, I'm not stupid. It's when you are mean to black people just because they are black."

"If you are mean to anyone who is different from you, then you are prejudiced. Our father is prejudiced, and he is mean to women too."

Mark's body stiffened against JJ's. His voice trembled. "Why are you saying bad things about Dad?"

"Because they are true. You can't tell me you haven't seen Dad be mean to Mom before."

Mark remained quiet a few moments. With a bit of shame in his voice he said, "I remember he pushed her once when they were upstairs arguing. It scared me."

"Mom tries to hide us from that. At least she did. She isn't going to let him do that any more."

There was silence between them while Mark quietly cried now understanding why they were really here. JJ pulled him close and held him long after Mark had fallen asleep.

The next day they were busy moving into the apartment Mathew found for them. It didn't go unnoticed by Karen that Mark was quieter than usual. She had heard the boys whispering in the bed the night before and was sure she had heard Mark crying softly. She wondered what had been said between them. Mathew and Greg were there helping move the furniture and getting them settled in. They finished and all went out to get some dinner. Karen was acutely aware that Mark was studying his uncle and Greg's interactions all day. The men were not overtly affectionate to each other in public but at the same time they did not hide the love they had for each other. Karen knew, sadly, this was definitely a different experience her boys had in their own home. She wondered what was going on in their minds. JJ was fine and was happier than she had seen him in a very long time. Mark on the other hand appeared to be struggling to sort things out in his mind.

After the boys went to sleep, Karen and Jamie sat on the apartment balcony talking. Jamie told her how much she respected Karen for making such a scary change in her life. It was Kate that had helped her to see she was responsible for controlling her own life by standing up to Jack.

Karen told Jamie she would understand if she chose to return home to Canada. She would hate to lose her but would book a flight home for her when she wanted to go. Jamie expressed how close she felt to the boys and to Karen and would like to stay as long as Karen needed her. It was a great relief to Karen that gave her the freedom to start looking for a new job. Karen told her the money from Jack would stop the moment he realized they weren't coming back. Jamie was fine with room and board for now. With Mathew's kind help, which she had every intention of paying back, Karen had also every intention of keeping Jamie's contract as it stood. They were both happy with their decisions.

Suddenly Mark appeared in his pajamas. Jamie excused herself and went to bed. "Hey, sweetheart, can't sleep?"

Mark sat down in the chair Jamie had occupied. He looked up at her questioningly. "Mom, is Dad a bad person?"

Karen didn't rush to an answer. Instead, she asked, "Why do you ask that question?"

"Because sometimes he can be really mean."

She was concerned how much of Jack's behavior he had witnessed, she hoped it was not as much as JJ had, with first-hand experience. Karen smoothed out the skin on his clenched fist. His hand relaxed. "Mark, there is good and bad in everyone. No one is perfect. It is important, however, for everyone to treat others with respect." It was time not to avoid his question. "Sometimes your father has trouble doing that."

Before she could say more, Mark stated, "Dad is prejudiced, isn't he?" He looked deflated. "That's wrong. Uncle Mathew and Greg are gay, and Dad doesn't like them because they are." Karen was surprised by his comment. Before she could respond, he continued. "Grandpa and Grandma are prejudiced too. Uncle Mathew is their son and they don't respect him either. That's wrong. I like Uncle Mathew."

Karen breathed a sigh of relief. "I'm so glad you do. Is there anything you don't understand or want to ask me about him?"

Mark looked so grown up as he stated emphatically, "I know he and Greg kiss and stuff. But it's okay for them; they are different."

"It is definitely okay for them. That is who they are. And they deserve respect from everyone."

Mark sat back in his chair and sheepishly asked his mother, "Did you leave Dad for good? So, we won't see him again." He started to cry.

Karen pulled him into her lap. "Mark, you can see your father anytime you want to. Remember I said there is good and bad in everyone. He is still your father. He loves you. It is okay to love him too. Whenever you want to visit him, you can." Having said that, her heart ached knowing Jack would send for him and push him off on her parents, or his, for the whole visit.

"I'll think about it for a while."

"You do that. And when you need to talk about it again, we can anytime you want."

"Mom, I respect you," he said, to show her how grown up he was.

She once again saw her son as the little, sensitive boy she knew. Her heart melted. "Mark, I respect you too for having such an open mind and for thinking things through."

Karen felt such a rush of relief as Mark headed back to bed. She knew the worst was over… for now.

# CHAPTER 9
## Ann

Her last patient of the day had been seeing Ann for six months now. He suffered from deep depression most of his life and Ann was pleased to see him making progress with his struggles. Ann related his feelings to that of her father's deep depression over the death of his wife and Ann's brother. Ann finished her notes and leaned back in her chair. She was overdue for a visit to her father and was thinking about when it would be a good time for a long weekend visit and when that would work with her schedule.

Kate knocked lightly and peeked around Ann's office door. "Hey, girl."

Ann looked up and smiled. Kate continued, "Peggy's car won't start, so I'm going to drive her home. I have a little more work to do so I'll be back. I'll lock the front door. Jerry's taking a look at Peggy's car."

Ann nodded. "I have a little more to do as well, bring me back a latte."

"Will do. Be back soon."

Ann pulled out her research notes to review for a patient she was seeing first thing in the morning. She settled in with her work and had quickly lost track of time. She glanced up at the clock at the same time she heard the front door open. It was after six. Having spilled her coffee on papers in the past, she rearraigned her work, anticipating the latte Kate was bringing.

Ann looked up to see a muscular forearm slowly pushing the partly opened door. Her heart began to race as she recognized the large tattooed cross on his inner arm. She instantly scanned the room looking for a possible weapon. Nothing came to mind for a defense. *Don't panic. Speak convincingly.* He stood at the door smiling at her. Ann forced a smile. "*Randy,* how nice to see you. You must have crossed messages with Meg. Her appointment isn't until tomorrow. Is her car in the shop again?" She prayed that he was buying her act and believed she didn't recognize him as being her rapist.

He didn't answer and just stood there looking at her. His stare was exactly like Meg had described, far away. His stare turned cold and menacing like the night of the rape. She knew she had to think fast. Ann saw his hand slowly move to the handle of a hunting knife in a shiv attached to his belt. Her mind began to race as self-defense class flashed before her. Stay calm. Don't let him corner you. Look for something for a weapon. She knew she had a much better chance of escape if she was in the waiting room closer to the door and elevator. Ann picked up the metal water pitcher. Holding it out toward him. She said, "I was just about to fill this." Her only chance was to get past him through that door and get into the waiting room. She controlled her shaking as she moved around her desk and came toward him. She couldn't swing the pitcher at his temple until he moved out of the door frame. Silently, she took a deep breath. She knew she had to take this opportunity even if it was risky. She stood directly in front of him and said with a smile, "Excuse me, the water cooler is in here," motioning toward the waiting room behind him. For whatever reason, he turned to the side and allowed Ann to inch past him. He smelled like sweat and cigarette smoke as he did that night in the garage. Her stomach lurched. She prayed she wouldn't vomit. She quickly stepped into the waiting room and stood by the water cooler. *God, where is Jerry!* She was afraid to bend over to fill the pitcher, making herself more vulnerable, nor did she want to take her eyes off of him.

As she hesitated for that split second, he spoke in a threatening voice. "What do you and Meg talk about?" The exit door was on the other side of the cooler and she knew he could easily reach out and grab her if she tried to run out.

She stood with the water pitcher in front of her. With as much authority she felt he could handle without setting him into a rage, she replied, "Randy, I can't talk to anyone about my patients and our conversations." His jaw set and his hand slowly moved up his leg to the handle of his knife still sheathed in its cover.

His eyes narrowed mockingly, and he said, "Well, there are always exceptions to the rules." He stated emphatically, "She won't be coming back here again, but you are still going to tell me." He smirked at her. He looked past her suddenly as Ann too heard the elevator stopping at their floor. She was terrified it was Kate returning and that she would be walking right into danger. Ann gripped the handle of the water pitcher and was prepared to swing at him the moment the office door opened.

A deep, angry voice was heard simultaneously as the door opened. "I told Kate to lock this door."

Rick took two steps back as Jerry entered the room. Two giant men stood looking at each other. Ann quickly walked around the cooler next to the door and took Jerry's arm. "Randy, this is my husband, Jerry. Honey, he is the brother of one of my patients."

Ann's message couldn't be clearer to Jerry. You could almost smell the testosterone in the room. Jerry's eyes were lasered into Rick's. Ann watched Rick lower his eyes to the floor and his shoulders slightly drop. It was a classical submissive behavior of a male in the presence of an alpha male. Men like Rick often felt their manhood threatened by other men. Violence and the controlling of women gave them back that power in their tortured minds. Jerry nodded toward the office door and said, "The office is closed; I'll walk you out."

Rick obediently walked out in the hall with Jerry. Ann heard the elevator door close. She dropped into a chair near the water cooler. Her whole body was shaking, and her head was pounding from the adrenaline. Her phone vibrated in her pocket and it startled her. She fumbled with it and saw a message from Kate. She was tired and changed her mind about coming back to work, she was home. Ann didn't even want to imagine what could have happened if it had been Kate and not Jerry who had walked in.

Jerry returned and examined the office door lock. "He picked the lock." Ann stood next to him as he showed her how he had gained entrance. "I got his license and the make of his car. From what you said about his sister, you already know who he is."

Ann corrected the information. "His name is Rick, not Randy. Rick Cross." Jerry looked confused but didn't interrupt. Ann continued, "He is a mechanic out of work and lives with his sister. He's the guy who attacked and raped me." Jerry's jaw set in anger; his hand clenched into a fist. She was glad that Jerry didn't ask any further questions that she professionally could not address. "Did he say anything to you in the elevator?"

"No, not a word. I played the jealous husband and told him I didn't like any men who weren't patients of yours, and to stay away from you. I stood next to his car and watched him drive off."

Jerry followed behind Ann's car and they made their way to the house. He parked and asked her to stay in her car until he checked out the yard and inside the house. He returned, opened Ann's car door for her. Matter-of-factly he said, "No new surprises were left." Ann asked Jerry to please not tell Nicky what had happened. It would serve no purpose but to frighten her more than she already was. They nodded in agreement.

The following day, Meg didn't show for her appointment. No message was left with Peggy at the front desk. Ann didn't really expect to see her after Rick's announcement that she would not be back. Ann worried that his declaration did not include violence to his sister.

## Karen

They had been so busy settling into the apartment, Karen felt she needed to check in with Ann since she hadn't spoken to her in a week. Thanks to Jamie, she had a few quiet moments to herself. She texted Ann asking how she was doing and if all was okay. Karen's phone rang instantly. It was Ann.

"Hi. I'm glad you called. So much to share." Karen proceeded to catch up with her on the news. Ann was so easy to talk to and the news came spilling out. She was already looking for work and checking out schools for the boys before summer was over and time for them to go back. JJ was starting ninth grade already and she knew that was a rough transition. Mark wasn't yet sure if he wanted to go back to Tucson. He missed his friends and Karen suspected he also missed his dad. She was praying he wouldn't but was preparing herself if he chose to go. She took a breath and said, "Listen to me go on and on. I didn't even ask how you are doing."

Ann laughed. "So glad you are being so productive and busy."

Karen noticed Ann had not responded to her question. So, she paraphrased, "So, what's up with you? Are you doing okay?"

Ann felt no need to share what had happened in the office with Rick. It had been two weeks since he made his appearance. Karen was safe in San Francisco for now, there was no need to frighten or worry her with the latest news of Rick's appearance at the office. "Good, all is quiet. Jerry is keeping a tight leash on me. I'm lucky to be able to pee by myself."

Karen was relieved to hear that, but she sensed that Ann was trying too hard to be cavalier and was holding something back. Ann continued. "Hey, listen, I decided I needed to get away for a few days and visit my dad up in Tahoe. I thought I'd fly into San Francisco and rent a car. Maybe we could get together while I'm in town."

Karen was genuinely excited. "That would be great! I'd love that."

"Great then, I'll get a flight out Friday night if that's good for you and I'll text you from the hotel when I check in." Ann would tell her about Rick's threat then.

"Sound great, we can have all day Saturday if you aren't on a tight schedule. Is Nicky coming too?"

"No, unfortunately she is too busy to get away from the hospital. So, it is just me. I'm looking forward to it. Talk soon."

Karen was already planning on introducing her to her family, which of course included Mathew and Greg. She would make sure they would be available for dinner Saturday night. That would give the two of them the whole day to really spend time together.

Karen got Ann's text Friday night as planned and she told her she would be at the hotel at ten in the morning. Jamie and the boys were planning an outing with Mathew and Greg and planned to meet the girls for dinner.

Ann waited for Karen in the hotel lobby, she was right on time. Without hesitation, they hugged. They walked around the corner and found a cute little café to have brunch. Karen looked up from her fruit salad and put down her fork. "You know, Ann, I don't want to spoil our day, but I can't help but think I wish Addie was here right now. We know nothing about her and it's like she never existed."

Ann's face saddened. "I know. I wonder who she was, we will never get a chance to know. There hasn't been any further investigation. It's considered a closed case."

Karen shook her head sadly. "I wish we could find a way to lead the police to… *him*."

Ann looked a little uncomfortable. "I have to tell you something. I wanted to do it in person." Ann knew it was time to tell Karen about the incident at her office. She hadn't allowed Jerry to tell Nicky or Kate and she was glad they weren't here to hear about what she was about to tell Karen. Ann ran her hand threw her hair nervously and said, "Rick broke into my office."

Ann told her what had happened, Karen was horrified. "Ann, I cannot imagine the fear you are living with daily. I feel so badly you are doing this on your own…"

Shaking her head, Ann interrupted her. "No, I am so relieved you and the boys are safe here. Have any more death threats come to your home?"

"No. I spoke to my mother just yesterday. She said it's been without incident for a few weeks now. I told her the boys and I are not coming back. She is not the raving type. She just told me I was making a big mistake and hung up. I'm sure Jack will be calling soon."

"How do you anticipate that going?"

Karen shrugged her shoulders. He is busy campaigning and until that's over, he won't do anything. Don't get me wrong, he will definitely be threatening me. Ann, I honestly don't care. I can't imagine he will want custody of the boys. Besides being their baseball coach, which he does only to look good in the community, he pays no attention to them and certainly won't want to be responsible for their care. He will complain about paying child support and brag to his colleagues that he does. Jack is all about Jack."

They continued to share their lives with each other. That horrible bond that had brought them together faded to the background for a much-needed rest. The last thing either one of them wanted was to talk about the rape right now. Karen was safe and Ann needed this opportunity to enjoy being out of the constant stress awaiting her back in Tucson. This new friendship was easy. They spent the rest of the afternoon laughing and feeling a freedom they had not felt in a very long time. They agreed that the day had passed much too quickly as they went to meet Karen's new family at the restaurant.

Ann felt instantly comfortable with Mathew and Greg. She could see why Karen adored her brother. He was a supportive and gentle man. It was obvious he was thrilled to have his nephews around him. Greg beamed in Mathew's light, and for that moment she missed Nicky terribly. After dinner, the boys were getting restless and Jamie took them back to the apartment while the others continued to get to know each other.

Ann was able to get a real feel for Karen's parents and husband and how she and Mathew felt growing up. She surprised herself by confessing her visit to her father would be difficult for her and how her great childhood changed when her brother died.

They were surprised at the late hour as the conversation continued effortlessly. Mathew and Greg took Ann back to the hotel. Ann and Karen hugged and promised to continue texting at least once a week. They wished that the circumstances that caused them to be in separate cities were different. They knew that their friendship was sealed, and it would always remain important to them both.

The next two days dragged by with her father. In her heart Ann knew the visit to her father really was about seeing how Karen was doing. Nothing had changed, he still preferred to prepare his owns meals and be alone, rarely going out. The first night at her childhood home she wandered around the house. Nothing had been moved, only dusted and replaced in the designated places her mother had chosen before her death. She slept in her old room, staring at the ceiling and feeling helpless in making a difference in her father's life. He had refused to take the anti-depression medication she wanted to prescribe for him. He just smiled at her and asked how she and Nicky were doing. It was painful sitting on the patio, silently looking out at the beautiful lake, knowing his walks along the shore were over for years now. She tried to convince him they should go out for dinner. He just shook his head no, and that was that. She filled the silent void by remembering how she and her brother loved playing and running in and out of the cold-water of Tahoe during summer break. She didn't share her fond memories with her dad because it only made him sad.

She drove to the Sacramento airport to return the rental and catch her flight home. Nicky's broad smile and hug greeted her at the Tucson terminal. She was home, and holding Nicky in her arms was what she needed to get her out of her funk over her father. She shared her great experience meeting Karen and her family. Karen had asked that next time Ann came to visit to bring Nicky for sure. Karen was looking forward to meeting her. Nicky smiled and said she promised she would take some time off as soon as she could, and they might head up to the Napa Valley and just relax for a few days. She said she would love to meet Karen from all Ann had told her about their visit.

Ann returned to the office the next day. It would have been the day scheduled for Meg's session, but it had been over a month since Meg stopped coming. Ann was hoping to hear from her, but there was nothing. She hoped that Meg was doing okay. With that thought, she looked in Meg's file and found her work number at the dental office. She stared at it a few minutes. *The hell with it!* She dialed.

"Dr Mason's office, how may I help you?"

'Hi, I wonder if Meg Cross is not busy with a patient, I could speak to her?"

"Oh, I'm sorry, she has been out of the office for a few weeks. She was in an accident and is taking some time off. Can I help you with something?"

Ann heart sank with the unexpected news. *What if… Oh God, he's hurt her!* "No, nothing thanks."

"Well, have a good day then."

Ann sat there debating what to do. She paced her office. Finally, she texted Jerry's phone asking him to come into her office. He occupied himself with his laptop most of the day in the office kitchen/lounge with a view of the front door. He knocked lightly at Ann's door and entered. He sat down on the couch and waited for Ann to speak. "Jerry, has there been any further signs of Rick while I was gone?"

Jerry being a man of few words said, "No."

"His sister hasn't shown up for her therapy in a while and I'm a little worried. The office receptionist where she works said she had an accident and was taking time off."

His poker face remained the same, only his eyebrows raised indicating to Ann that he too was concerned. "You want me to do a little snooping?"

"Maybe we should."

"After I get you home tonight, I'll check it out."

Jerry went back to his comfy lounge and Ann tried to regroup and concentrate on her next patient.

The following day, Jerry reported that he had gone by Meg's house. It was quiet and all the curtains and blinds where shut. Rick's car was parked in the driveway next to Meg's little red Cooper. The next week he checked the house daily. Both cars were still parked in the driveway and he sat for a while and watched. There was no activity.

The following week, Ann decided after work she would have Jerry take her over to the assisted living facility where Meg had placed her mother. Maybe she could shed some light on what was going on. Jerry waited in the car while Ann went in and asked to see Mrs Cross. The receptionist looked up at her and smiled. "I'm sorry, dear, Mrs Cross no longer stays with us. Her daughter has taken her to her house to live."

Startled be the news, she asked, "When did this happen?"

"About a week ago now."

Ann started to panic. *They cannot both be in the house with that man!* "Was it her daughter Meg that picked her up or her son?"

"It was her daughter. She was looking forward to having her mother home with her."

*Did Rick force this change?* Ann returned to Jerry in the car and reported what she had found out. He said he would check out the house again tomorrow and maybe ask the neighbors a few questions. He didn't have to.

The next morning Ann settled into her office and began to prepare for her first patient. Peggy stood at the door and announced that Meg was on the phone and asked to speak to her. Ann grabbed her phone. A little too desperately she asked, "Meg? Are you okay?"

She didn't answer, but instead, she enquired, "Dr Weise, could you fit me in today?"

Ann did not want to be interrupted by another appointment and told Meg to come at the end of the day. She wanted to give Meg as much time as she needed. Meg arrived at Ann's office dressed neatly with her hair brushed and in place. For the most part she looked fine, but Ann could see her makeup was heavy in an attempt to hide some bruising. She took a seat and started to talk right away. "You told me, that whatever I say in here is just between us. Is that still true?"

Ann nodded. "Yes, that is true."

Meg released her handbag from her clutching fingers, putting it beside her as if to say she would then stay to talk. "I have had trouble sleeping for a couple weeks now. I killed Rick. I need to tell you about it so maybe I can sleep again."

Ann's first reaction was shock, but she needed to understand if Meg was talking figuratively or she had really killed her brother. She cleared her throat and calmly said, "Why don't you tell me what happened? Start at the beginning."

"The day before I was to come to your office, Rick said I wasn't to go back to see you. I told him that you were helping me with my stress. I lied and said it was stress from work. He said it again, that I was not to go back to see you. I tried to reason with him, and he…" Meg hesitated a moment and her hand unconsciously touched the bruise along her jaw line. She continued with, "He beat me up pretty badly and left me in the kitchen. He left me there and went into the living room and turned on the television." Meg began to cry softly and wiped away some tears with a tissue Ann handed her. "Thank you." She continued as Ann watched her relive it. "I was afraid to leave the kitchen, so I stayed in there and finally fell asleep on the floor. I couldn't go to work looking like that, but I was afraid to stay home too. So, the next morning while he was asleep, I got in the car and just drove around for hours thinking about what I was going to do. Randy was no longer part of

Rick, nothing left. If I appealed to Randy, it just made him angrier.

When I walked in the door, he was at me again. Screaming at me that I better have not gone to see you. He knew what you and I talked about and that he was going to kill you this time for good. Like the night before I couldn't calm him down. He threw things around the room and then he—" Now she began to sob. Ann went to her, wrapping her arms around her, holding her while she cried. Feeling Meg's helplessness, Ann felt her own tears streaming down her face, knowing what was coming. Finally, Meg controlled her shaking body. With intense fury she shouted, "Dr Weise, he dragged me into the bedroom by my hair and raped me!" Ann flashed back to the warehouse and like it had happened yesterday, she saw Rick dragging Karen by the hair into the warehouse. Ann shuddered. Meg continued, "Thank God I passed out." With indignation and outrage, she said shouting, "He raped me!"

Ann's head flooded with memories of the night in the warehouse. Her anger raging for both of them. Ann waited a few moments and asked her, "Are you able to continue, or do we need to stop?"

Meg tightly gripped Ann's arm. Pleadingly she said, "I have to tell you everything! I have to."

Ann patted her back. She totally understood, firsthand, Meg's need to finally release her feelings. "Okay. When you're ready, I'm here to listen."

Meg sat for a few minutes to gain control. She continued and admitted, "He has beaten me in the past. It was infrequent while I could still get him in touch with his Randy." Her voice quivered "He never raped me before. There were times he would look at me in that *way,* but he never crossed that line before. This time he was totally out of his mind and I thought he was going to kill me. I was desperate. I did nothing the next day but stay in my room until he left the house. I was terrified he was coming for you next. I ran to the store and I bought almond flour, and any other nut flour I could find." Ann was confused why Meg was talking about nut flour now. She waited and hoped for the connection to what happened next. Meg continued speaking. "He got home, and I acted like nothing had happened when he got back. I went into the kitchen made dinner and a cake with the mixed nut flours." She looked at Ann and lowered her eyes briefly. Quietly she said, "He is allergic to nuts." Ann remembered her mother had briefly mentioned his food allergies during their visit. *Oh, now it was starting to make sense.*

Ann refused to show her shock, keeping a calm face as Meg continued once more. "He ate a big piece of the cake and went into anaphylaxis shock at the dinner table. I couldn't watch, I just couldn't. I went into my room and closed the door. All those years of saving him and being in fear, I just couldn't do it any more. It couldn't have been more than fifteen minutes, he was gone. I called for an ambulance. I told the EMTs that he brought home the cake from a friend's house and he must have thought it was safe to eat. I told them he was allergic to nuts and I had just gotten home and found him there."

Ann watched as Meg released all the bottled-up tension and stress from her body. It must have been such a relief to finally get this all out. Ann suddenly realized that she too had been released from all her fear as well. Her body and mind were free of tension. A heavy weight she had been living under had disappeared. She felt she could finally breathe freely.

She wanted to reassure Meg. "I am so glad you came here today. We are going to work through this together. It's going to be all right. Tomorrow, I want you back here and we will begin to get some clarity on all this."

Meg took a deep breath, blowing it out slowly. "I start back to work tomorrow. It will have to be a late session."

Ann nodded and said, "I'll be here. Meg, I have a favor to ask of you. You had mentioned that Rick said he had killed Addie Carson and a hiker. Could you bring in an item of his that would have his DNA?" Ann could see Meg was leery. "The reason I ask is, it might help Addie's closed case. It could bring closure to the hiker's family too if he did kill her."

Shamefully she uttered, "What if they start to investigate Rick's death?"

"This will be handed over to the police, from me, along with a threatening note I received. I need to know it was from Rick because a friend of mine received a similar threat." Ann leaned forward with a serious expression. She knew she was about to commit an *impermissible* professional breach and taking a big chance by becoming personally involved with a client. Ann knew this moment would have to be the end of sessions with Meg, but she would make sure Meg's therapy wouldn't stop. She continued. "Rick raped both of us and Addie Carson as well. He may have killed an unknown hiker. We need to find closure for Addie, my friend, and that hiker's family."

Meg's eyes looked like saucers and she began to tremble. "Oh, dear God!" Her mind was racing. There was silence for a few minutes, digesting all that had been shared. Meg's face was set in a look of determination that Ann had seen in her before. "Dr Weise, you… you too need closure!"

Ann smiled at her. "That is what we are going to do together. We are survivors. *If* you choose to come back tomorrow with Rick's DNA samples," Ann emphasized, "*Only if you want to,* I can assure you it will be handed over by me. Rick has made two separate threats to me since the rape. If the police choose to follow through and check it out, those families will be notified that the cases have been solved. Unfortunately, I suspect there are other women out there who have been victims of his violence. His DNA may help many others. There are, I'm afraid, many more women out there not as brave as you were. I believe, if this is the case, the police will be happy to know he is off the streets without further investigation. If there is need for investigation, it will come back to me. As I said before, what has been discussed between us is privileged information." Having said this, Ann leaned back in her chair and hesitated briefly before speaking again. "I am seeing a wonderful woman therapist for months now. She is straightforward and has helped me deal with the rape. I intend to keep seeing her. By sharing all this information about your brother, I have broken an oath as a therapist. The process we work under, cannot work with what I have done today. With your permission, I would like to have you work with her. You are at an important place in your therapy and I am very confidant she will be a good match for you. This is important. We both need to heal." Ann took a cleansing breathe and added, "Meg, she can be trusted. I give you my word on that."

Meg had listened intently to all Ann had said. "I have a lot to think about. I feel like you are more of a friend then therapist to me. I realize why you can no longer work with me, but it makes me sad."

Ann's face broke out in a genuine smile. "I will miss you too. You need to know that you have been very helpful with my struggle as well. I have been inspired by your strength. Please begin to recognize that in yourself."

They embraced, and Meg gathered up her purse to leave. As she opened the door to exit, she turned and said, "Thank you."

"You are welcome. I hope to see you tomorrow." Ann then added, "Meg, throw out the nut flour."

# CHAPTER 10

Ann called Nicky at work to let her know Rick had died and she and Karen were finally free from this horrible journey they had been put through. Ann knew she had more work to do with her therapy, but Nicky finally could relax. Nicky didn't yet know the details but didn't ask, not knowing if Ann was free to disclose her patient's confidence. Ann would call Kate and Brad for a celebration dinner. Kate was thrilled with the news and they planned their celebration for the next night.

She then told Jerry. His face remained stoic, never showing his emotion. He did, however, attempted to show his dry humor. "I guess that means I'm out of a job."

Ann laughed, "Well, you are invited to a celebration dinner tomorrow night."

Nicky got home and after telling her basically all the details, it was too late at night to call Karen. They finally went to bed, but Ann lay there thinking about all that had happened. She wondered if Meg would return to her office tomorrow.

She got into the office early. Ann was surprised to see Meg sitting in the waiting room. Ann gestured for her to come into her office. "Dr Weise, I hope you don't mind that I came in so early, but it's my first day back at work and I wanted to give you this before I chickened out." She pulled a Ziplock bag from her purse and handed it to Ann. It contained a hairbrush, toothbrush and a few cigarette butts.

Ann took the bag from her. "Thank you, Meg. Hopefully you have just helped a lot of women and their families." She went to her desk, retrieved Marty's business card and handed it to Meg.

Meg didn't reach for it, instead she said, "I have lived with fear and stress since Rick was born. This is the first time in my life I feel totally free from that. I have my mother home with me and safe. We are both going to enjoy our lives now. I have gotten over many obstacles in my life that he has caused, I can get over this too. I just want to move on."

Ann got it. She too believed she could just move on. It took her months to start her own therapy. Ann reached out with the card again. "Please take it. You may have flashbacks and anger with everything you have been through. Just in case you change your mind." Almost begging her she said, "Please think about it seriously. I will call you as soon as I know anything about the DNA results.

Meg took the card. "I want to thank you again for all you have done for me."

Ann glanced at the clock. She knew Meg's job was close by and she would have no trouble getting to work on time. "Meg, can you sit for a minute. I promise I won't keep you long?" Meg sat down in the chair she was comfortable with over a year now. "Way back when, you told me Rick had a bad accident that caused him a long recovery in the hospital, it wasn't Randy obviously who found him. Could you tell me about that day?"

Meg looked up at her and nodded. She understood that Ann needed all the puzzle pieces. "You and your friend were the women in Rick's garage that night, right?"

"Yes, as well as Addie Carson." Ann realized that Meg had time to put two and two together after yesterday's discussion.

Shaking her head, she said, "I don't want to even think about what you went through." Then she began. "My car was in his shop for repairs. My friend at work had been picking me up and taking me home. That morning, Rick told me my car was finished. So, after work I took my friend Helen to dinner for taking me back and forth for almost a week. I asked her if after our dinner she could drop me off at his garage to pick up my car so she wouldn't have to pick me up for work in the morning. I had a second set of keys. We remained talking for a while and she needed to get home. We saw that the garage lights were on, so she dropped me off and left for home. The garage door was lifted enough for me to duck under. I was going to just tell him I was picking up my car. I saw him lying on this mat bleeding badly. I cut his restraints and wrapped him tightly in a blanket I had in the trunk of my car. That's when I saw blood all around the floor and…" Ann watched Meg's face cringe in recall. "That's when I saw that poor woman in the back of the garage and cut like he did to animals as a child." She swallowed hard and continued. "I got him in my car and took him to the Tucson Medical Center Emergency."

Ann already knew the answer, but she still asked. "Did you go back to the garage?"

"Yes. Once again, I listened to Rick. He told me to go back. He said there was a can of gasoline back at the garage and I had to burn down the place to get rid of the evidence." She looked up at Ann. "I still saw some semblance of Randy in him. I spent all those months of his recovery trying to get him back. I came to realize during that time that Randy was quickly slipping away. I was losing the battle, yet I still wasn't able to kill him. He was a rabid dog and still I could not put him down."

Silence remained between them for a few minutes. Ann was first to speak. "You and I spent many months talking about the guilt feelings you felt each time you wanted to kill him. You still have guilt issues you need to work out now that you have. This and watching you relive that night are only a small part of the flashbacks of a lifetime yet to come. Please think seriously about seeing Dr Stein."

Meg closed her eyes for a moment and nodded. "I will, I promise."

Later at the celebration at Brad's favorite sports bar, Ann was able to tell the most important people in her life how it all unfolded. Well, almost all of it. Enough to keep Meg safe from the authorities, explaining he had eaten a cake, made of nut flour, it was his allergy to nuts that killed him. They were somber but relieved that Karen and Ann were finally safe. Nicky squeezed Ann's hand. "Although I never, and most likely never will, meet your unnamed patient, I am so grateful for her strength and bravery in handing over her brother's DNA."

Jerry was the only one at the table that knew who Meg was. He and Ann exchanged knowing glances. In a rare moment, he shared his thoughts. "I retired as a cop before I started bodyguard work. I saw a lot of injustices when I was a cop. Our justice system let a lot of evil men back on the streets. Until society sees women's abuse and rape issues more seriously, it's good to know there are still some very strong women out there who find their own strength. Maybe that's why some men are intimated by them and continue to let them fight for themselves." His comments were expressed with deep emotion. Ann suspected it came from a very personal place. That had been the first time they heard Jerry speak more than short sentences.

The somber silence that lingered after his comments was interrupted by the news playing above them on one of the many televisions in the bar. Jack Michaels was their newest councilman. Ann said she really needed to call Karen with the latest information she had gotten from Meg this morning. She excused herself to the quiet sidewalk to make her call. Karen answered right away. "Hi, are you okay?"

"Yes, I am. We just heard on the news. Jack won."

Karen chuckled. "Unfortunately, someday you might have him as your governor. I shudder to think. Actually, I'm glad he won. He, I'm sure, will be on such a high he won't even care when divorce papers are served to him tomorrow. It's good to be able to deal with the mundane. It's you I'm worried about. Any more news?"

"Actually, there is. For now, you just need to know Rick was found dead. The nightmare is over." There was a gasp at the other end of the phone and shocked silence. "Are you still there?"

Karen felt sudden relief. "My God. How did it happen?"

"That is a long story that I hope to tell you in person. Nicky and I are planning a getaway retreat up to Napa for a few days. Is the invitation for a visit still open?"

"Absolutely! I have great news too. I was feeling so guilty that I left my job telling my boss it was a family emergency and never called him back. His name is Doug and he is a great guy. So, I finally called to tell him I took the boys and left Jack and I was now relocated in San Francisco near my brother. He said if I needed a job reference, he would be happy to give me one; then he said, he has a friend here in the city who is a child advisory attorney. He said she needed an office manager. I called and lo and behold, I have a new job.”

Ann was so thrilled for Karen. “That is incredible! I am so proud of you. I’ve watched you find your strength and confidence and it makes me so happy for you.”

Karen’s voice became serious. “You know, Ann, in some ways it took that horrible night to wake me up. I was so scared to even leave the house. I was scared to fight back at Jack’s and my parents’ disrespect and indifference. I was setting poor examples for my sons. I was at the lowest most frightening point in my life. You and Kate came into my life and along with that came the strength to do what I had to. Knowing that animal is dead is the most freeing feeling in the world. I know that might sound harsh but it’s true.”

“It isn’t harsh, and it is true. When Nicky and I come up, remind me to tell you what Jerry said tonight. They are coming out of the restaurant, so for now I have to go. Love you.”

“Love you too. Hug Kate for me. I can’t wait to finally meet Nicky.”

It was Jerry who delivered Rick’s DNA to the police. He had friends in the police department that respected him. He made sure they followed through with checking. As Ann had suspected, Rick’s DNA matched evidence from Addie’s apartment as well as the hiker found on the trail. They continued to check similar closed cases and found two more of his victims. Jerry was also very convincing that the death of Rick was an accident due to his allergy and didn't need investigating.

# Meg

Meg placed a cup of tea in front of her mother and answered her phone. "Hello? Yes, this is Meg." She listened for a few minutes. She smiled and said, "Thank you again, Dr Weise. The news of no investigation takes a load off of my mind. I think I can start to move forward now. By the way, Dr Stein, is almost as good as you. We are exploring a decision I have to make very soon." Meg held her hand under her budding baby bump and glanced at the lit Catholic prayer candle on the counter next to a Rick's photo. She was glad that Ann was not here to see the pain on her face or know how she was struggling with deciding what to do about Rick's child inside her. This innocent child conceived in rape. Ann did not need to be burdened further with Rick's violence and the consequences it left with the survivors. "Thank you, I'm proud of myself too. Have a wonderful evening, sleep well."